fly

on

the

wall

also by e. lockhart

the boyfriend list

e. lockhart

fly on
the wall

how one girl saw <u>everything</u>

delacorte press

Published by
Delacorte Press
an imprint of
Random House Children's Books
a division of Random House, Inc.
New York

Visit us on the Web! www.randomhouse.com/teens
Educators and librarians, for a variety of teaching tools, visit us at
www.randomhouse.com/teachers

Library of Congress Cataloging-in-Publication Data
Lockhart, E.
Fly on the wall : how one girl saw everything / E. Lockhart.
p. cm.
Summary: When Gretchen Yee, a student at the Manhattan School for Art and
Music, wishes she were a fly on the wall of the boys' locker room, she never expects her
wish to come true in such a dramatic way.
ISBN 0-385-73281-3 (trade : alk. paper) – ISBN 0-385-90299-9 (Gibraltar lib. bdg. :
alk. paper) [1. Artists–Fiction. 2. Interpersonal relations–Fiction. 3. Metamorphosis–
Fiction. 4. Flies–Fiction. 5. High schools–Fiction. 6. Schools–Fiction. 7. New York
(N.Y.)–Fiction.] I. Title.
PZ7.L79757Fly 2006
[Fic]–dc22   2005005702

The text of this book is set in 11.5-point Baskerville BE Regular.

Book design by Angela Carlino

Printed in the United States of America

March 2006

10 9 8 7 6 5 4 3 2 1

BVG

for Daniel,

because this is my first romance

part one

life as an

artificial redhead

friday. I am eating alone in the lunchroom.

Again.

Ever since Katya started smoking cigarettes, she's hanging out back by the garbage cans, lighting up with the Art Rats. She bags her lunch, so she takes it out there and eats potato chips in a haze of nicotine.

I hate smoking, and the Art Rats make me nervous. So here I am: in my favorite corner of the lunchroom, sitting on the floor with my back against the wall. I'm eating fries off a tray and drawing my own stuff–not anything for class.

Quadriceps. Quadriceps.
Knee.
Calf muscle.
Dull point; must sharpen pencil.
Hell! Pencil dust in fries.
Whatever. They still taste okay.
Calf muscle.
Ankle.
Foot.
KA-POW! Spider-Man smacks Doctor Octopus off the edge of the building with a swift kick to the jaw. Ock's face contorts as he falls backward, his metal tentacles flailing with hysterical fear. He has an eighty-story fall beneath him, and–
Spidey has a great physique. Built, but not too built. Even if I did draw him myself.

I think I made his butt too small.

Do-over.

I wish I had my pink eraser, I don't like this white one.

Butt.

Butt.

Connecting to: leg . . . and . . . quadriceps.

There. A finished Spidey outline. I have to add the suit. And some shadowing. And the details of the building. Then fill in the rest of Doc Ock as he hurtles off the edge.

Mmmm. French fries.

Hell again! Ketchup on Spidey.

Lick it off.

Cammie Holmes is staring at me like I'm some lower form of life.

"What are you looking at?" I mutter.

"Nothing."

"Then. Stop. Staring," I say, sharpening my pencil again, though it doesn't need it.

This Cammie is all biscuits. She's stacked like a character in a comic book. Cantaloupes are strapped to her chest.

Her only redeeming quality.

"Why are you licking your Superman drawing?" Cammie tips her nose up. "That's so kinky. I mean, I've heard of licking a centerfold, but licking Superman?"

"Spider."

"What?"

4

"*Spider*-Man."

"Whatever. Get a life, Gretchen."

She's gone. From across the lunchroom comes her nasal voice: "Taffy, get this: I just caught Gretchen Yee giving oral to some Superman drawing she made."

Spider. Spider. Spider-Man.

"She *would*." Taffy Johnson. Stupid tinkly laugh.

Superman is a big meathead. I'd never draw Superman. Much less give him oral.
I haven't given anybody oral, anyway.

I hate those girls.

Taffy is doing splits in the middle of the lunchroom floor, which is just gross. Who wants to see her crotch like that? Though of course everybody does, and even if they didn't, she wouldn't care because she's such a unique spirit or whatever.

I hate those girls, and I hate this place: the Manhattan High School for the Arts. Also known as Ma-Ha.

Supposedly, it's a magnet high school for students talented in drawing, painting, sculpture or photography. You have to submit a portfolio to get in, and when I did mine (which was all filled with inks of comic-book characters I taught myself to draw in junior high) and when I finally got my acceptance letter, my parents were really excited. But once you're here, it's nothing but an old, ugly New York public school building, with angry teachers and crap facilities like any other city public school—except I've got drawing class every day, painting once a week and art history twice. I'm in the drawing program.

Socially, Ma-Ha is like the terrible opposite of the schools you see on television, where everyone wants to be the same as everyone else. On TV, if you don't conform and wear what the popular kids are wearing, and talk like they talk, and act like they do—then you're a pariah.

Here, everyone wants to be different.

People have mohawks and dreadlocks and outrageous thrift-store clothes; no one would be caught dead in ordinary jeans and a T-shirt, because they're all so into expressing their individuality. A girl from the sculpture program wears a sari every day, even though her family's Scandinavian. There's that kid who's always got that Pink Panther doll sticking out of her jacket pocket; the boy who smokes using a cigarette holder like they did in forties movies; a girl who's shaved her head and pierced her cheeks; Taffy, who does Martha Graham–technique modern dance and wears her leotard and sweats all day; and Cammie, who squeezes herself into tight goth outfits and paints her lips vampire red.

They all fit in here, or take pride in not fitting in, if

that makes any sense—and if you're an ordinary person you've got to do *something* at least, like dye your hair a strange color, because nothing is scorned so much as normalcy. Everyone's a budding genius of the art scene; everyone's on the verge of a breakthrough. If you're a regular-looking person with regular likes and dislikes and regular clothes,

and you can draw so it looks like the art in a comic book,

but you can't "express your interior life on the page," according to Kensington (my drawing teacher),

and if you can't "draw what you see, rather than imitate what's in that third-rate trash you like to read" (Kensington again),

then you're nothing at Ma-Ha.

Nothing. That's me.

Gretchen Kaufman Yee. Ordinary girl.

Two months ago I capitulated to nonconformity-conformity and had my hair bleached white and then dyed stop-sign red. It cost sixty dollars and it pissed off my mother, but it didn't work.

I'm still ordinary.

I take literature second period with Glazer. I rarely do the reading. I don't like to admit that about myself; I'd like to be the person who does the reading—but I don't.

It seems like I've always got some new comic to read on the subway, and the homework for drawing is more interesting.

In literature, I can't concentrate because Titus Antonakos sits next to me at the big rectangular table. He's an Art Rat, meaning he's one of the boys in the sophomore drawing program, group B. He's delicious and smart and graceful and hot. White skin, with high cheekbones and messy dark hair. Lips like a Greek statue—a little too full for the rest of his face. He's got a retro Johnny Rotten look; today he's wearing a green vinyl jacket, an ironic "I heart New York" T-shirt, jeans and combat boots. He's thin to the point that he's off some other girls' radar, but not mine.

He is absolutely on my radar.

Titus.
Titus.
Titus.
Touch my arm by accident like you did yesterday.
Notice me.
Notice me.

"Gretchen?" It's Glazer.

"Huh?"

"Vermin." She's obviously repeating herself. She sounds annoyed. "The word. I asked you to define it."

"It's a bug, right?" I say. "Like a cockroach."

"It can be," says Glazer, smirking. "Most people do assume that Kafka had his protagonist, Gregor Samsa, turn into a cockroach. That's the standard interpretation of 'The Metamorphosis.' But if you all turn to page five, you'll see that the word Kafka used in German—and the word in our translation—is not *cockroach* or *bug*, but *vermin*—a 'monstrous vermin,' Kafka says—which can be taken to mean any kind of animal, especially those that are noxious or repellent in some way: rats, mice, lice, flies, squirrels."

No idea what she is talking about. I just know the story is about some guy who turns into a bug.
Whatever.
Titus.
Titus.
Titus.
God, he smells good.

"Titus?" Glazer, calling on him. He actually put his hand up.

"Doesn't it also mean disgusting *people*?" Titus says. "Like you could say people who—I don't know—molest kids or steal from their mothers—they're vermin."

"Absolutely." Glazer lights up. "And by extension, you sometimes see the word used as a derogatory term for the masses—for large groups of ordinary people. Or for prisoners. It expresses contempt. Now: why would

Kafka use such a word to describe Gregor's meta-morphosis?"

Titus did the reading.

He just seems good, somehow.

Like the core of him is good when the core of other people is dark, or sour. Like he'd do the reading even if no one was checking, because he cares about stuff.

I wish he didn't hang with those Art Rats. I have class with them every single day, but I can't figure those guys out.

Because they're boys, I guess, and because they try so hard to seem slick and sure. They're nice one minute and cruel the next.

And with Shane around all the time, I can't talk to Titus. At least, I can't talk and make any sense.

Truth: with Shane around I can't talk to anyone.

The bell. "Finish through page sixty for Monday and enjoy the weekend," calls Glazer. A rustle of books and backpacks.

"Hey, Titus." My voice sounds squeaky. (Shane, thank goodness, is out the door.)

"Yeah?" His mouth looks so soft.

"Oh, I–"

Hell. Was I going to say something? Did I have something to say?

Oh hell,

oh hell,

he's looking right at me, I've got nothing to say.

"Do you–"

What?
What?

"–do you remember what the Kensington is?"
Titus bends over to pick his pencil off the floor. There's a strip of skin between his shirt and the top of his jeans in the back. I can see the top of his boxers. Plain light blue. "Sketch three sculptures of the human body at the Met, remember?"
Of course I remember. If I had a single bone in me I'd ask him to go there on Saturday with me.

I should ask him.
I should ask him.
I should ask him.

"Oh, right," I say. "That's it. Thanks."

Oh! I am a coward!
Spineless, boneless, vermin girl.

"Sure. See you in gym." I try to smile at him but it's too late. He's gone.

Later that afternoon, Sanchez the gym teacher makes us play dodgeball, which leaves bruises all over my legs. I'm not that fast, and I get hit a lot. Titus hits me twice.

"Do you think it means something?" I ask Katya after gym, sitting on the locker room bench in a towel.

Katya is naked in the shower like that's a normal way to have a conversation. She's washing her hair like she's just everyday naked in front of people.

Well, we *are* everyday naked in front of people. Gym is five days a week, shower required. But anyway, Katya is having a naked conversation like it doesn't even bother her, which it obviously doesn't—even though she's not built like a model, just regular.

The locker room is so cramped and tiny that I can feel the warm spray of her shower water on my knee as I'm sitting on the bench.

"It would have meant something if we were sixth graders," says Katya, scrunching her eyes as she rinses out the shampoo.

"Like what would it mean?"

"You want to hear me say it?" She's laughing.

"Yes."

"It would have meant that he liked you back."

"I didn't say I liked him," I mutter.

"Oh please," Katya says, ignoring my point, "that's very sixth grade. You know, how boys were always teasing the girls they liked, pulling their hair. But we're way too old for that crap now. So I don't think it means anything if he hits you with the dodgeball. Sorry."

Katya is always such a realist. She's soaping her underarms like she's alone. I could never do that.

I make a quick dive out of my towel and into my bra and a T-shirt from the second Spider-Man movie, covered with pastel dust. "I didn't say I liked him," I say again.

"Oh, don't give me that."

"What? I'm analyzing the cruel and particularly complicated sociodynamics of sophomore dodgeball."

"No, you're not." Katya is drying off now. In the next row over, annoying Taffy is stretching and showing off her dancer's body while listening to our conversation. I hate this tiny-ass locker room.

"What, it's that obvious?" I ask.

"It's all over your face, all the time," Katya says, grinning. "Titus, Titus, Titus."

I'm blushing. I can feel it. And my Chinese half makes it so that once my cheeks go pink, they stay that way for hours.

Katya never turns pink. Broad, Russian American face and a lumpy nose and long pale brown hair—you wouldn't think she'd be pretty if you made a list of her features, but somehow she is. She's mysterious. You can't read what she's thinking.

"Well, he's better than the others," I say, conscious of Taffy in the next row, trying to sound less obsessed.

"Whatever."

"He is. Let's be objective. He's cuter than Brat Parker. Nicer than Adrian Ip. More interesting than Malachy."

"What's wrong with Malachy?" Katya sounds annoyed.

"He never says anything. Like having his ears pierced makes him so slick he doesn't have to talk."

"You don't have to be so mean about everyone, Gretchen."

"I'm not being mean. I'm doing an objective comparison of the Art Rats."

Which isn't true. I *am* being mean.

I feel mean. I don't know why. This school is making me evil, maybe.

"It's not objective. It's *subjective*." Katya hooks her bra behind her back. "It's just what you think, not the truth."

"Don't bite me, Katya. I'm only talking."

"Well, you're talking about people you barely know."

"I know them. They've been in practically every class with me all year. I know Shane."

"We all know you know Shane. Enough with Shane." Katya gets into a dress she made herself on her mother's sewing machine.

"Wanna get a slice?" I try changing the subject.

"Can't. I've got to pick the monsters up at day care."

I wish she didn't have three little sisters. Wish she didn't live an hour-fifteen away from school on the F train, all the way in Brighton Beach.

"You're always busy these days," I say, and it comes out pitiful and whiny.

"That's life, Gretchen," snaps Katya. "I've got responsibilities. I'll call you later."

She's out the door. My only friend, really.

I can't count Shane, even though we said we'd be friends after last October.

We're not, obviously.

Not friends.

Just people who groped each other for a few weeks at the start of this year, when he was new and sat in front of me in math. One day, he wrote me a note about this nose picker sitting in the front,

and we wrote notes back and forth about boogers,

which led to notes back and forth about other stuff,

and he ate lunch with me and Katya,

and put funny sketches in my locker,

and we were friends. I thought.

But one day Shane walked out of school with me when classes were over,

and got on the subway with me,

and went home with me, without me even asking him.

He kissed me as soon as we got in the door. We made out
on the couch, when my parents weren't home,
　　and watched TV on the couch together when they were.
　　After that, we made out in the hallways of Ma-Ha,
　　by the boat pond in Central Park,
　　on the corner by the subway stop,
　　and in the back of a movie theater.
　　People saw us. And he was my boyfriend. For a little.
　　Now, he's just someone whose mouth I stuck my tongue in,
　　someone whose spit got all over me and I didn't mind at
the time.
　　Now, he's an alien being,
　　just like all the rest of those Art Rat boys—
　　or even more than the rest.
　　It goes to show that if you only have two friends in a
whole godforsaken poseur high school, you shouldn't start up
kissing one of them, because three weeks later he'll say he
doesn't feel that way,
　　whatever way that was,
　　didn't feel like drooling on me anymore, I guess is what it
meant—
　　and he'll say, "Hey, it was fun and all, but let's cool it
now, yeah?"
　　and "You know we'll always be friends, right? Excellent.
Let's hang out sometime, Gretchen, that would be great,"
　　only not with kissing,
　　and not with it meaning anything,

and then, when it comes down to it, never actually hanging out,

and never being friends again, unless people ask and then we both say:

"Yeah, we had a thing going for a few weeks there, but then we both decided we would just be friends."

Only he's the one who decided.

And we're not friends, not anymore.

Now he's got the Art Rats and goes out with Jazmin, and little Gretchen Yee isn't worth his time, like she was when he was new in school and lonely.

Hell.

I'll get my stupid slice of pizza by myself, then.

So I get some pizza and walk thirty blocks home instead of taking the train. That way, I don't have to hang around my house too long with Ma, who's supposed to be writing her dissertation but never actually is, and who's usually cleaning something and primed to quiz me about my day when I get home.

I slink into my room and read the new *Spider-Man* comic, plus a couple back issues, for an hour. Then Pop comes home from work with a sack of takeout, and we eat tofu in black bean sauce and fried rice cakes and soup dumplings, and it tastes so good I don't even think about anything for a few minutes—and then Ma clears her throat and says: "Gretchen, your father and I have something to tell you."

I wonder if the school called because of that day I skipped out and went to the movies, but then Pop says: "You know things have been difficult around here."

"It's hard to know the best way to say this . . . ," adds Ma.

And it hits me. They're getting a divorce.

They talk about it for a while, saying
they're so sorry,
they went to see a marriage counselor,
they tried everything,
they can't get along together anymore,
they just don't know what to do, and
they're going in to sign the papers tomorrow.

I won't have to listen to them yelling.

I won't have to prick up my ears as I fall asleep because I'm not sure if it's the TV or the two of them starting in on each other again.

I won't have to try and talk them out of arguing in the Kmart
or Number One Noodle Son
or the subway.

And I won't have to hear them say stuff to each other like
"You weren't very considerate when we were getting into bed

last night and I was trying to talk to you about the thing that happened right before dinner, do you know what I'm referring to?" or other crap like that before I go out the door to school,

and then have to have the unresolved parents-fighting ache all day, cold in my chest.

"Gretchen bubbee, we're going apartment hunting this weekend!" Ma is trying to sound bright, changing the subject to something more pleasant.

"What?"

"You and me. Tomorrow. Looking at apartments. Then we can talk about paint colors."

"Isn't Pop supposed to move out and get a bachelor pad?" I say. Bitchy.

"He *is* getting one," says Ma, bitterly. "We're selling the apartment."

"It's not a bachelor pad." Pop does that thing with his voice where it's clear he's intent on keeping his temper. "Hazel, don't go putting ideas in her head. Gretch, it's a studio."

"Where?"

"West Twenty-fourth Street. You can come see it. Tell me what I should buy to fix it up."

"See it?" I say. "What if I want to live with you?"

(Not that I do. But *come see it*? To your kid?)

"Oh. Um. It's a studio." Pop stands up and starts clearing the table.

"And how come you have it already and you're just telling me this stuff now?"

"I told you she'd be mad," says Ma. "I told you to get something bigger."

"Gretch, don't be like that." My dad, coaxing.

"Like what?"

Suddenly I'm almost crying.

How weird,
like you could think you were relieved and then you're crying,
like you didn't even know you were sad.

"I'm funding two households now," says Pop, as if we're both incredibly stupid and he has to spell stuff out for us. "A studio is what I can afford. What do you expect me to do, Ma?"

Why does he call her Ma? I'm the one who calls her Ma.
If I ever have a husband I am never letting him call me Ma, even if we have fourteen children. It's probably why they're getting divorced. If he'd have just called her Hazel everything would still be fine.
There's a hole in my shirt.
Why would I get a hole right there near the bottom edge? It's not like anything is rubbing on there.
I wonder if I should darn it.

If I keep thinking about the hole I won't cry,
darning is definitely not sexy,
would black thread look okay on a dark blue shirt? Or do
I have to go to the drugstore and get blue?
I can't believe he's moving out
moving out
moving out.
Now no one will scramble eggs with dried fish from
Chinatown and stink up the whole apartment,
no one will leave the toilet seat up,
no one will play Sinatra and try to make me dance,
or drag me to the dog run in Central Park to hang out
with the dogs even though we don't have one,
or buy me comic books and hide them from Ma,
or watch TV in his ratty bathrobe in the middle of the night
when he can't sleep and wake me with his too-big laughter.
Don't cry don't cry don't cry.

"I'll miss you, Gretchen," he says, coming over. "I hope you know that."

I haven't hugged him in so long.

Wait.
He smells like cigarettes.
I didn't know he smoked. Since when does he smoke?
He doesn't. Maybe he's got a girlfriend who smokes.
Oh hell.

It's obvious.

Obvious, obvious, obvious.

Crap.

My dad has a girlfriend:

I can't believe I didn't notice before.

He has someone else; that's why all this is happening. It explains the late nights and the long business trips and the tie he said the cleaners lost. My father has got some chain-smoking chippie on the side and he's leaving our family so he can cavort around town lighting her cigarettes for her.

I

can't

believe

he

would

do

this

to

us.

I run into my room and slam the door.

My room is a wreck. Here's what's on my shelves:

A stack of collectible *Spider-Man* comics in plastic sleeves, six piles of ratty old comics, which include Spidey, some *Fantastic Four, Batman* and *Dark Knight, Punisher, Incredible Hulk, Doctor Strange,* a few *Savage Dragon, Witchblade, Grendel,* stuff like that. Oh, and *League of Extraordinary Gentlemen.*

A half-open box of old pastels,

three years' worth of *Fangoria* magazine,

some travel souvenirs from Hong Kong, where I went with Pop last year,

an old laptop computer that doesn't work anymore but seems like it's too valuable to throw out,

thirteen Pez dispensers (including Tasmanian Devil and Peppermint Patty),

a semi-huge collection of action figurines including G.I. Joe, Betty and Veronica, Rosie the Riveter, Spidey, Jar Jar Binks (someone gave him to me), and a few vampire-type guys,

four jars full of little plastic characters from Asia, left over from a phase I had when I was fourteen: Bean Curd Babies, Hellcats, Devil Robots, Snorkin' Labbits and Anti-Potato Head.

A big box of silly makeup from when I was younger: glitter eye shadow and blue lipstick, plus ordinary pink lipsticks Ma gave me when they were nearly worn down,

all my old picture books,

all my old chapter books,

a paper doll collection,

seven plastic baby dolls, all white babies except one
little Asian one, none of which I've played with for years,

thirty-one stuffed animals (grimy),

five jewelry boxes, all given to me as gifts by my
Chinese grandmother, all empty.

Oh, and on my floor:

dirty clothes,

clean clothes,

clothes I tried on and didn't wear,

"The Metamorphosis," which I still haven't cracked,

art supplies,

tablets of drawing paper,

shoes,

paper clips, all over where they spilled last week,

eighteen plates of plastic Chinese food, which I just
started collecting,

tissue packets, partly open,

and half an old bagel, wrapped in paper.

I, Gretchen Yee, am a pack rat.

A pack vermin.

Divorce. Divorce. Divorce.

I have to do something to make me stop thinking about it.

*Divorce. And my cheating, lying father—I have to get him
out of my head, too.*

*I'll do my drawing assignment—not the one where I have
to go to the Met—but the one I was supposed to have handed in*

today. *"Draw something or someone you love. Put your emo-tions onto the page, but draw from life, or from a photograph."*

Okay, what do I love?

My stuff. My figurines, my comics, my old toy animals. But there's too much of it all to draw. And everyone will laugh at me if I do that, anyhow; everyone but Katya.

So not them.

What do I love? What do I love?

Ma knocks once on the door and leans in. "Gretch?" She sounds apologetic. "Are you okay, bubbee?"

"Yeah. I'm doing my Kensington."

"Listen. The appointment with the realtor is at nine a.m. tomorrow."

How did she get an appointment so fast? It's not like you can call up realtors after working hours on a Friday night and arrange to see apartments.

Oh.

Duh.

She's known about this for weeks. They only now told me. Ma has been on the phone with realtors for ages, planning our move, and is only telling me now, at the last minute.

"And Gretch?" Ma sits down on my bed. "Just so you know. The place we're gonna move to, it'll be smaller than this one. I mean, money's tight now, and for a two-bedroom in Manhattan, they're asking a lot. But you'll like this one we're seeing tomorrow. It's in Chinatown, and there's an old claw-foot bathtub."

She's not only been on the phone with realtors, she's been to see apartments already. She's even picked one out.

"So. You might want to start thinking about what you want to keep, and what you want to throw away." Ma executes the should-be-patented Hazel Kaufman switch from sympathetic mother to critical nag.

"What do you mean?" I ask her.

"We've got to sort through your junk, Gretchen. We can't bring all of this"—she waves her arm to indicate my stuff—"to the new place."

"But I need my stuff!"

"You don't need all of it. You don't need most of it."

"Ma!"

"Gretch, you have to throw it out. We're starting fresh."

"*You're* starting fresh," I say. "I'm only moving with you because I'm legally obligated."

It came out worse than I meant.

"Don't be smart with me," Ma snaps. "Pop and I are going through a difficult time. The least you can do is be cooperative."

"Fine." I yank off my jeans and get into bed in my T-shirt. "I'll pack my stuff."

"There's more to her than that. She's an incredibly kind person. Anyway, she called me last night after you went to bed and said that she and Gary were supposed to go on this trip to a tiny island in the Caribbean, a resort—and now Gary can't go because of some work obligation. She's furious at him. He's always doing this."

"And?"

"She knows what a hard time I've had separating from Pop, and she said she could switch Gary's reservation over to me, if I wanted. It's all already paid for."

"She's taking you on vacation?"

"She's offering. Only we'd have to leave on Friday afternoon. This Friday. Would that be okay, bubbee?"

"But Pop will be at that toy convention thing in Hong Kong."

"I know, but you stayed on your own that weekend last fall, didn't you? When we went up to the Kesslers'?"

"Yeah."

"Gretch, I wouldn't ask but I'm so exhausted I can't tell you." She's shoving an enormous fry into her mouth and washing it down with coffee.

"When does Pop get back?" I ask.

"The following Saturday. So you'll be a week on your own."

"Eight days."

"Okay. Eight days. And then I'll be back a couple days after that! It's this amazing place. There's a spa where you can get massages, and there are no cars on the whole island. Everyone goes around by bicycle."

She's so bright, talking about it.

She loves the beach.

She's never been to the Caribbean.

And Ma hasn't looked bright for a long time, now that I think about it.

Sometimes I hate my dad. Even before this affair with the chippie,

and even before this divorce,

it seemed like all he did was make Ma unhappy.

Maybe they're just too different. Because he's Chinese American and she's Jewish.

Or because he owns a small toy company and she's trying to be a scholar.

Or because she's a blabbermouth and he's quiet.

Or he's a man and she's a woman.

"Sure, go on and get a tan." I try to smile. "I can deal."

"We can leave the extra key with Ramón down the hall." Ma squeezes my hand. "And I'll take you grocery shopping and leave you money and all that."

"Okay."

"You sure you'll be all right, on your own?"

"Absolutely."

●

Aside from the übervillains and murderers and vermin
wandering the streets. Yeah, I'll be fine.

I escape from Ma and head up to the Metropolitan Museum of Art to do my Kensington homework. There's beautiful stuff in the Jaharis Gallery of Greek art, and I sit down with my pad and begin sketching a statue of a naked man reclining with a bunch of grapes.

This is hard. The stone makes the body look different; softer. Plus he's lying down. Superheroes never recline on their elbows, draping themselves around like that. They're always in action.
How do I make it look like stone?
How did the sculptor make stone look like skin?
Eraser,
eraser,
dust off—
hell.
A smudge.
Shoulder, shadow, forearm, shadow;
this one is coming out okay.
Maybe Kensington will actually like it. I do draw bodies better than most people in class. That's not conceited, it's true. Katya's bodies always look like they're stiff, like she's drawn a doll instead of a person.

Do men really look like this?

This guy has no hair.

I may not have seen any naked boys up close, but I've walked through Chelsea in the summer when all the men have their shirts off, and even people who wax themselves stupid still have hair on their arms, or their underarms, or somewhere. And lots of the nonwaxers are seriously furry.

Was it an aesthetic decision—like the sculpture looked better with no hair—or is it just too hard to carve chest hairs out of stone? Or were they waxing in ancient Greece?

Thank goodness I don't have to draw a gherkin, that's all I can say.

Fig leaf.

Titus is Greek. Titus Antonakos.

Titus.

Titus.

I wonder what he looks like naked.

"—I was thinking about basketball next year but I don't know. I don't actually like it that much." I hear a voice from the back of the room.

Titus! Could he be here, doing his Kensington assignment?

Don't turn around.

Don't turn around.

"Do we *have* to be on a team?" the voice continues. "What's the deal?"

32

"That's what I heard: everyone has to. But whatever—it's better than gym. And it's good for college." That's definitely Adrian Ip.

"I can't think about college already," says Titus.

"You just don't want to play a sport, fag." I can hear the sound of Adrian socking Titus on the shoulder.

I hope they don't see me.
No, I hope they do see me.

"Hey, isn't that Gretchen Yee?"

"Hair like that, who else?"

"Shut up!" Titus sounds like he's socking Adrian back.

They slide onto the bench next to me, pushing my pencil box out of the way.

"Naked man, eh?" jokes Adrian.

"My specialty," I sneer, heart beating fast. "What's up?"

"You doing the Kensington?"

"Looks like it." Me, trying to be slick.

"We saw Taffy and Cammie drawing Egyptian stuff in the other gallery." Titus opens the zipper on his backpack.

Are they gonna stay here? And like, do the Kensington with me?

●

He gets out his sketchbook. "Cammie's looked good, actually."

"Cammie always looks good," says Adrian, smirking.

"I meant the drawing, you vermin."

Titus remembers vermin, *too. I like that.*

"I'm just a red-blooded Korean love machine," says Adrian. "You can't miss that Cammie milkshake."

"Whatever. I wasn't in the mood to do those Egypt ones, so we came over here." Titus shrugs.

"What he means is, they wouldn't talk to us." Adrian laughs.

Uh-oh. Does Titus like Cammie, then? Or, please no, Taffy?

"That's true," Titus giggles, "they wouldn't. But only because Ip made some crap comment."

"What did he say?" I ask.

"It's not for your ears." Titus busies himself digging around for a pencil.

"Why not?"

"It was disgusting, that's why."

We are having a full-out conversation. Me and Titus, and Adrian.

●

"Adrian, what did you say?" I push.

He holds his hands up in self-defense. "I'm not saying it again. I got in too much trouble last time."

"Try me. It's not like I'm some innocent."

"Oh, don't worry," he says, cracking a smile. "I
don't think *that*."

What does he mean by that*?*
Has Shane been talking about me?
*What do those guys know about me and Shane? It's not
like we went so far.*
Would Shane talk about it?
*Oh hell, would he talk about that time in the back of the
movie theater?*

"Ip was being a half-wit," says Titus. "And now he's
learned his lesson and he's keeping his trap shut."

"That's true," confesses Adrian. "Hey, Titus, what's
up? Are you staying here and drawing this naked guy?"

Titus answers without looking at him. "I'm thinking
yeah. I'll see if I can do better than Gretchen."

Does that mean he thinks I draw well?
Or he thinks I draw badly?

"I'm not drawing any naked dudes," says Adrian.
"Way too gay. Come on and look for some ladies
with me."

"Oh, all right, booty master." Titus laughs. "Your wish, my command." He shoves his pencil back in his backpack and tucks his sketchbook under his arm. "See you, Gretchen."

"Bye."

And they're gone.

What did he mean, do better than Gretchen?
What did he mean, booty master?
What did Adrian say to Cammie?
"Hair like that," Adrian said. Does that mean stupid fake red hair, or sharp electric sex-goddess hair?
And what did Shane say about me?

Later Saturday night, Ma is banging pots around in the kitchen, cleaning up after a strained family dinner. Pop is letting her do it, sitting on the couch with the remote in his hand. He's handsome, my dad. He doesn't look forty-five.

"It's starting, Gretch," he says to me as I clear the last of the dishes from the dining table. "Don't you want to come sit down?"

No. I don't want to sit down.
He's unfaithful.
He's leaving for the Hong Kong toy exhibition tomorrow.

He's leaving our family for a bachelor pad in Chelsea.
I am not watching Star Wars *on TV with him.*
I don't care how hot Harrison Ford used to be.

"I gotta call Katya."

"Didn't you call her earlier?"

"She was out. I have to talk to her about something."

"She'll call you back when she's in."

"I don't think her mother gives her messages."

Why hasn't she called me back? I need to dissect the whole Titus/Adrian conversation and she hasn't been in all day.

Which is weird, since she said she was watching her sisters.

I go in my room and speed-dial her. Mrs. Belov picks up, sounding frazzled, and says Katya is still out. I leave another message. Then I try to sort through my stuff, which Ma has been on me about like six times since we first discussed it, even though it was only yesterday.

I start with the baby dolls. I haven't played with them in years, but I remember all their names: Plastic Baby, Mini-Baby, Yellow Baby (this one with yellow hair), China Baby, Rollo, Lala and Pinkie. They stare up at me with hard eyes full of longing. "Don't throw us away," they seem to be saying. "You can't shove us in a garbage bag and send us to the Salvation Army shop. How will we breathe in the bag? And what will happen to us once we get there? We'll be split up and go to different houses, and the children there will be mean to us, and we'll never see each other again. You can't do that to us, Gretchen. We love you."

So I leave the babies alone, and skip the stuffed animals for the same reason, and start going through my clothes. A T-shirt with a stain. I could throw that out, but I could also wear it when I go running—not that I've gone in two months. But still. It's something to wear.

I put it back in my closet.

A pair of cords with a hole in the butt. But they're good cords, so soft, and I could patch them.

They go back in the closet, too.

A red vinyl micromini I've been too shy to wear. But maybe I'll get up the nerve, like if Titus ever asks me out. Besides, with money being tight now, it's not like I'll be able to get another one if I let this one go and then change my mind.

So then I look at the comics and the books, but the comics I have to keep, because I need them for my art and I'm always rereading them, and besides, it's a collection. And the picture books I know I should give to my cousin Rachel, who is only three, but I love most of them, and it seems to me that an artist should have a collection of picture books anyhow, for inspiration. I find an extra copy of *Harold and the Purple Crayon,* and a book called *The Berenstain Bears and the Messy Room,* which is a big guilt trip about cleanliness that Ma bought me in hopes that I'd learn to pick up my stuff, back when I was six—and I shove those in a bag for Rachel. But the rest, I'm keeping.

Now the chapter books. I might reread them. They're not for babies. Like I loved the Chronicles of Narnia, and *The Wolves of Willoughby Chase,* and all those Tamora Pierce books, and Artemis Fowl and Harry Potter. Who's to say I won't look at them again? I don't have a social life. I've got to have reading material.

Then I tackle the Pez dispensers, and actually shove them into the bottom of the big black garbage bag before pulling them all out again, because they could be worth something someday. I read on the Internet that there are actually Pez-collector *conventions,* and what if there's one here that turns out to be worth like two hundred dollars, only I've sent it off to the landfill?

Same with the action figures. I can't get rid of them. Some of them I only bought last month.

The art supplies I need. The makeup, likewise, though I hardly ever wear any. But what if I suddenly start? What if I wear some lipstick one day and Titus looks at me with new eyes, riveted to my gorgeous, honey-colored mouth? I'll need to have the rest of this stuff at my disposal.

In the end, I manage to shove the broken laptop into the garbage, along with the old bagel, the ugliest of the jewelry boxes and two books of paper dolls where the dolls are missing so there's no one to put the clothes on. That's it.

I can't throw anything else out.

Ma will be furious. She'll say I'm mired in junk, we need a new start, there won't be anywhere to keep all this stuff in the new place, what am I hanging on to it for anyhow, the movers cost money, don't I know that, and they charge by the hour?

I can't think about it. My room is a catastrophe, now that I've taken nearly everything off the shelves. I know I should straighten it up, but I somehow feel comforted by all the piles of stuff surrounding me. Like these objects are loyal, they're mine, they're not going away. They want me to keep them and love them.

So I go to sleep with the baby dolls all on the bed, around me.

Monday in first-period drawing, Kensington sticks student art on the corkboard with pushpins so she can critique it publicly. It's an exercise in humiliation, and we have to go through it several times a week. Today, we're discussing last week's assignment to "Draw Something You Love," which is part of our general focus this term on portraiture and drawing the human body, only Kensington is also trying to get us to draw *feelings* and *character,* so now and then we have to do a personal drawing like this, which is supposed to help us invest our portraits with drama and pathos. I handed mine in late, because I just did it on Sunday afternoon and gave it to her this morning, along with my statue drawings.

"There's a lot of emotion here," says Kensington, starting with Katya's picture. Kensington is dressed all in black, with bleached blond hair and heavy black glasses.

Katya drew baby Ella, which is sweet, but obvious. Loving your little sister. Ella looks lopsided. She's sleeping in her parents' big bed, dwarfed by the pillows and a floral duvet cover. The fabric looks stiff.

"You draw from the heart," Kensington goes on, "and anyone would fall in love with that baby from your depiction. But you had some trouble with shading the nose, I see." She starts talking about techniques for drawing facial features, and I look at the other pictures.

A souped-up motorcycle; that'll be Shane. The bike is his older brother's. He always draws with a soft touch like that. He made the cycle so shiny, it glows.

The electric guitar. That's Adrian. He's such a poseur. I bet he never played guitar in his life and just drew one because a guitar seemed like a slick-guy thing to draw.

A box of fancy chocolates, half-eaten, wrappers strewn all over. The paper cups look real, which I know must have taken

forever. Paper is hard to draw. The chocolates make me think
Cammie; she seems like the type to have a big box of candy like
that. But Cammie could never draw wrappers that well. It's
gotta be Malachy. He's a candy man. And he draws with that
narrow line.

"Bradley Parker—which is yours?" Kensington has
finished with Katya and is moving on to the next victim.

That small, freckled white woman with glasses must be
Brat's mother. She looks a bit like him—washed out with a
pointy chin and a tired look around the eyes.

"You've done one of the most difficult tasks in portraiture." Kensington gushes. "You've captured the ec-
centricities of your subject without descending into
caricature. This woman is absolutely specific, and even
a little comical, but she is drawn with respect and deli-
cacy. Nice work, Bradley."

Brat smiles, but as always he seems slightly nervous, like he's not settled into his seat.

"Titus Antonakos," says Kensington. "You drew a
human heart?"

Titus
Titus
Titus

"My dad has these medical textbooks."

"You worked from a photograph?"

"Uh-huh."

"All right. Shading is getting better. There's a feeling of"–Kensington stops, pushes her glasses up her nose–"curiosity, a clinical eye. I'm looking for the emotion in this image. Class, what do you see?"

"It's icky," mumbles this girl Margaret, who hardly ever says anything.

"It's so graphic," Cammie breathes. I bet she just wants Titus to look at her.

"Graphic, how?" Kensington.

Cammie purses her lips in thought. "Gory. Like a horror movie."

"Is that what you're getting at, Titus?" Kensington asks him. "Is this heart a violent image?"

"Not exactly." Titus scratches the back of his neck.

"Can the image be clinical and violent at the same time?" Kensington prods.

No one answers.

She goes on: "Does anyone see how this drawing answers the assignment, to draw something you love?"

No answer.

"Anyone?"

Silence.

"It's the opposite of love." Me. Talking without planning to.

"Hmm? How so?"

"People think of hearts when they think of love, but a heart is a bloody organ in the body. It doesn't have any emotions. It's like a metaphor for love that has nothing to do with what love actually is."

"Oh?" Kensington looks at me as if asking me to go on.

"So the picture's like loving the bare truth about love, not the crap that people think is love from Hallmark cards and chick flicks." Everyone's staring at me now. "Or it's about there being no love, not in the body. Like saying love is in the mind, or the eye–but not in the body at all. 'Cause look at that heart. There's no love there."

Hell. Why did I say all that? It didn't even make sense. It's like two different answers that don't match up with each other.

"Is that what you're getting at, Titus?" Kensington asks.

He blushes. "Something like that. Yeah, actually. That's what I meant."

"Well then. Good work."

He liked what I said.
He did.
And after class he will stop me in the hall and say, "You really understand me, Gretchen," and I'll smile in an attrac-

tive way and he'll touch my hair and our hands will brush against each other—and then it won't matter if people are walking by, he'll put his hand on my chin and kiss me, and from then on we'll—

"Gretchen Yee," says Kensington. "I'm sure we can all guess which is yours."

Everyone chuckles at this. Even Katya.

Shane laughs outright.

Maybe I shouldn't have laid it out comic book–style, in panels. I know that drives Kensington crazy. But I wanted to get that swoop where Spider-Man swings past the straight lines of panels, over the panels, out of the picture with his foot nearly up in your face and his left hand way in the background, holding on to the thinnest thread of webbing—to land in poor Gretchen Yee's hell-messy bedroom in the bottom panel of the page, late at night, where he rescues her from her tiny dark self and her insignificant life.

"All right, then. You love comic books." Kensington. "What a surprise. That's easy for all of us to see from your work so far this year."

"Yeah, but—"

"Gretchen," she goes on, "I thought I made it clear that I can't judge your progress if you continue to draw in this stylized manner. It's been obvious since the beginning that you've got an admirable command of human musculature"–another laugh–"but you're not going to develop your own style if you keep imitating the hacks who draw for the Marvel corporation."

But look at the drawing, Kensington. Look at the story.

"I can't judge your line, your shading, I can't judge anything when you draw this way. It's like bringing a synthesizer to a violin lesson."

But can't you look at what I draw for the drawing it is? Not for what it isn't?

Can't you tell me how to fix the foreshortening on Spidey's foot, or get the shadows right in poor Gretchen Yee's bedroom, illuminated by the moon?

And don't you want to find out what I love? Don't you even want to look at what I actually drew?

Because it's not that I love comic books. Sure, I love them, but that's not the point.

I love the idea of the big life–the life that matters, the life that makes a difference. The life where stuff happens, where people take action. The opposite of the life where the girl can't even speak to the boy she likes; the opposite of the life where the friends aren't even good friends, and lots of days are wasted away feeling bored
and kind of okay,
like nothing matters much.

I drew a picture of the big life. Spidey's is so big he bursts through the panels. And he's swooping in to take that little me—small, angry, impotent me—and yank her out of her room full of action figures and out into the large world where she should be living.

So maybe she'll do something for once.

I love that idea, Kensington. And if you'd only look at it, it's more interesting than a guitar or a box of chocolates.

Tuesday and Wednesday are uneventful. Pop leaves for Hong Kong, and it's a relief, since he and Ma have been sniping at each other every time I leave the room. One time, the day before he leaves, he smells like cigarettes again, which makes me wonder if he is bringing his girlfriend on the business trip with him. But I don't speak about it, and Ma doesn't either.

Then on Thursday, Titus comes up to me in the hall.

"Hey, Gretchen," he says.

"Hey yourself," I say.

"What's up?"

"With me? The usual. Random acts of violence, media saturation, teenage angst, utter mayhem."

I sound like an idiot. But what else am I gonna say? My parents are getting a divorce?

I'm practically flunking drawing and literature?

My best friend's barely speaking to me and changes the subject when I ask her where she was on Saturday night?

I think about you all the time and I want your body?

"Oh, yeah," he says. "Ha ha."

"What's up with you?" I ask.

He rubs the back of his neck. "I, well, Taffy said something, and, um, can I talk to you for a minute?"

"Sure."

Oh hell. Taffy, in her skintight leotards, has been talking about me behind my back? Saying what—that I give oral to my Superman drawings?

"I mean—"

"Wait," I cut in, before he goes any further. "Just let me say that Taffy is a half-wit."

"She—"

"Promise me you won't believe a word she says."

"Come on, Gretchen."

"No, I mean it. If Taffy is saying stuff about me, it's completely wrong."

"Oh." He looks a bit shocked. "All right then, whatever. She's actually nice if you get to know her."

He thinks she's nice? All she ever does is sneer at me like I'm a vermin.

"I didn't know you guys were friends," I say, trying to sound casual.

"We're not, not exactly," he mumbles. "We've just known each other since grade school, and—"

The bell rings for the next class. "Sorry," I say. "I'm having an off day. I'm sure Taffy's fine, she's just not my type."

"I've gotta get to class," Titus says. "If I'm late for lab again, I'll have to go see Valenti." (Valenti is the principal.)

"Later," I say. And he's off down the hall.

Hell. I clearly just ruined any chance I ever had. I've shown him my bitter ugly personality, said mean stuff about his childhood friend, and—

But why was he talking about Taffy, anyway? He said she said something. But what?

Something about me licking that drawing?

Something about me and Shane?

Something about what a freak I am? Or what an ordinary nothing I am?

Oh crap. I remember:

She knows I like him.

She was listening to me and Katya in the locker room the other day.

I bet she told him, and he wanted to find out if it was true.

And I told him that whatever Taffy says about me is completely wrong.

friday morning, Ma yells at me for fourteen minutes straight about the piles of stuff that are still all over my room, which I had promised to take care of before the end of the week. I make a few excuses, explaining how I tried to get rid of it, but I need it all, I really do—but then I give up trying to interrupt and simply time her rampage, sneaking glances at the clock on my desk. The only way to make it through.

"Don't take your anger at Pop out on me," I finally tell her, rolling my eyes at the ceiling. "It's obvious you're really upset about something else, not my stupid room."

"Don't give me psychobabble, young lady," Ma snaps—and her face looks angrier than I've ever seen it. Honestly, it's scary. "If you want psychobabble," she continues, "start analyzing your own bedroom."

"What?"

"You heard me. An anal-retentive inability to let anything go—does that ring a bell with you, Gretchen? Living in mess so bad you can't find anything you ever need—shall we say, what? Deliberately self-sabotaging? Or shall we discuss your collections, which any junior psychoanalyst would label borderline obsessive? Or your constant lateness? Or your bad marks in literature? Hey, we could have a whole conversation about learned helplessness, if you want to start psychoanalyzing each other."

I've obviously crossed some line. She's never yelled at me this way before. Usually, it's "Clean up your stuff, why don't you do what I tell you?"

"Leave me alone," I spit back. "I'm a teenager. I'm supposed to be messy."

"*No one* is supposed to live like this," Ma says, climbing over piles of stuff to make her way out of my room. "I don't know what we did wrong with you, I really don't."

And she bursts into tears, leaning her forehead against the doorframe.

I stay sitting on the bed for a bit, scared to go pat her on the back because she just said all these horrible things to me and they're starting to sink in,

and they seem kinda true, hellish as that is,

and I don't want her to start saying any more of them because I honestly don't think I can take it—

but eventually I scrounge a packet of tissues out from under my bed and offer them to her. She takes a handful and blows her nose, loudly.

"I'm sorry, Gretchen," she sniffs. "I shouldn't say those things to you. They're not true, they're not what I

51

think, I—with your father gone this time, everything seems different. It's not like the other times he's been away on business. More like he's left for good."

"Yeah," I say.

"And I'm so overwhelmed with organizing the move and I have to hand a chapter of my dissertation in to my advisor, and it's late, and I . . . I guess what you said hit a nerve. About me being mad at Pop."

"It's okay," I say as I walk to the kitchen to get her a drink of water.

But it's not okay. She can't unsay the stuff she said.

Am I self-sabotaging?
Or borderline obsessive?
What did she mean, learned helplessness?

I fill up my backpack, including the self-portrait I drew for art class today, and put some Vaseline on my lips. I kiss Ma goodbye and give her this pair of funky green sunglasses I bought on the street for nine dollars, a present for her Caribbean vacation. "I have to get on the train."

She gets all weepy again and snuffles into my neck as she hugs me, and says she's sorry four more times about the yelling, because she won't see me again until she gets back in ten days. She leaves money on the dining table, and shows me a long note she's written detailing which neighbors have extra keys, her flight information, Marianne's cell phone and where Pop is in Hong Kong.

And I leave.

On the subway, I'm trying to read my social studies homework when this really old man—I mean, he's like ninety-five—stumbles as he's heading toward the seat next to me. He sits full-out in my lap, like a baby, and I can smell his cigar and old-person smell as I catch his arm and help steady him. "Pardon, pardon," he says.

"That's okay." I smile.

When he's stable again, I help him into the seat next to me. We nod at each other, and I feel funny going back to my homework after what happened. He puts a tiny, wizened hand on my arm. "You never expect what you'll be at the end of your days," he whispers.

"What?"

"When I was young I thought I'd be young forever."

"Uh-huh," I say. He's so small and gnarled up, he seems like a gnome—or a fairy.

"Now here I am," he continues, "and my legs don't work good, and my eyes don't see good, I'm hunched over. You'd never believe I used to be an ice dancer."

He seems like he wants a response. "I believe it," I say.

"I took my wife ice dancing every weekend at Rockefeller Center."

Now he might be lying. "I bet you were good at it," I offer.

"I learned when I was a boy. We lived in Vermont. You know where Vermont is?"

"Sure," I answer, though I've never been there.

"Lake froze over in the winter," he continues. "Everybody knew how to skate. It was like walking. You learned when you were a baby."

"I've never done it," I say, though I've watched the skaters spinning around at the rink in Central Park.

"But you see the ice dancing on TV, right?" he asks. "When they have the Olympics?"

"Oh, yeah."

"What are you, teenager?" he asks.

"Sixteen."

"You think you'll be like this forever, but you'll change before you know it," he tells me. "Change before you know it."

"I'd love to change," I say. "Sixteen is horrible."

"No, no," he says, the way old people do when they're thinking about being young. "Sixteen is a treasure. You treasure it."

What does he know about my life that he thinks I should treasure it?

For all he knows, I might have abusive parents,
or be pregnant by some rapist,
or have some horrible wasting disease.
I might be an orphan, or a crack addict, or—
But the truth is I'm none of these things.

I force myself to smile back at him. "This is my stop," I say, standing up. "Have a nice day."

"Goodbye." He pulls a folded-up newspaper out of his pocket.

I dart out of the train and push through the crowds to the stairs. On the way up to the fresh air, I feel a squish underfoot and look down to see my flip-flop in a pile of white goo. It's all over my heel and the bottom of my shoe.

Hell, what is that stuff?
Could be gel-type shaving cream,
or industrial radiation waste,
or some nasty liquid insecticide,
or beef aspic.
It burns my foot.
Maybe it's vomit from someone who's only been eating oysters;
or a dead jellyfish,
or the waste of some enormous subway cockroach.
Ugh.

I yank off my cotton sweater and use it to wipe everything clean, and run into the first bodega I see when I get out of the subway. If I buy something, they'll give me a plastic bag that I can put my slime-covered sweater in, so it doesn't touch any of the other stuff in my backpack.

The bodega is tiny; it seems to deal mainly in lottery tickets, pervy magazines and gum. In the back, there's a cooler full of ice and bottled soft drinks—lots of which I don't recognize. They don't carry Coke or Snapple or any of the usual stuff. Just grape soda, celery soda, orange, coconut and fruit punch. I grab a celery one because I like its green color. I pay for it, and a packet of tissues, and ask for a plastic bag.

Outside, I finish wiping off my foot with a tissue and shove the gook-covered sweater into the bag.

What a day. Three dramas already and it's barely eight a.m. I open the soda and drink it as I head up the steps to Ma-Ha. It has a strange, overly sweet taste, and I toss the half-empty bottle in a trash can and slide into drawing as the bell rings.

by eight-fifteen, everyone's self-portraits are up on the board. Kensington is yammering on about Taffy's picture, which shows her bare feet on a wooden floor, like in a dance studio. They're covered with blisters and

Band-Aids. It's not that bad, actually. Better than I would have expected from her.

A fly is buzzing around the room.

Poor beastie. Trapped in here with no snacks and no fresh air. How did it get in?

The windows are always closed and you have to get a teacher to unlock them if you want one open, because some idiot jumped out a second-floor window a few years ago and broke her leg.

Titus's self-portrait looks like a skeleton. Like he sees himself as all face and no body.

Katya's is pretty good. It's her with her three little sister-monsters, all clinging to her and pulling on her clothes. She got her own expression just right: like she loves those kids to death, but they're making her insane—her hair all bedraggled.

Shane made himself look like a guy with secrets. Lots of black, it's really dark. I don't think of him that way at all. He seems like he doesn't think about stuff—he's all surface and no substance.

Well, that's not fair. Maybe I'm just mad at him.

I thought he had substance in October.

Brat's portrait is funny. He did himself squashed up against a piece of Plexiglas, so his face is all splayed out in queer shapes.

Adrian's is dull, which is surprising to people who don't

have drawing with him because he seems like he's got so much personality; too much personality, even. You'd think his draw-ings would reflect that, but they don't.

Malachy did a profile; it has a nice line. He was honest, too—you can see the texture of his skin in the picture. He's not bad-looking, but he drew every little mole, zit and pore.

Cammie made herself look pretty.

And me. Well, I did what Kensington wanted, and I won't have to listen to another harangue about my shal-low, imitative comic-book vision. I went for soft fine lines and a loose style—exactly what Kensington likes the most. A total capitulation to the art teacher's demands.

In books, the teacher is always right, and the hero-ine learns something. If this were a book about my life, I would have had some big realization doing this as-signment. I'd have broken through my wall of resist-ance and suddenly experienced drawing in a new way—more honest, more fulfilling. My high-art self-portrait would reveal so much more about me than my cheapo comic book stuff ever could. It would be hon-est, true and emotional.

But that isn't what happens.

I have drawn the ordinary, ordinary girl I see every day in the mirror,

so Kensington won't humiliate me again,

so Shane won't laugh.

And I look okay in the picture,
and it looks pretty much like me,
but there are no real clues to who I am, inside.
Looking at the picture makes me feel ashamed.

"Gretchen, we're seeing some effort from you," says Kensington, finished eviscerating Brat for his gimmicky attempt at humor.

"Uh-huh. I thought about what you've been saying." Me. Talking crap.

"Yes, you're getting more honesty in your work, and a more relaxed line," she says.

That poor fly is buzzing around Kensington now, and she's swatting at it.

Ooh, she hit it,
but it's still alive.

I hate it when people are mean to animals. That's why I don't eat meat,
or wear fur,
but the truth is, what really gets me is seeing someone leave a dog in a hot car,
or step on an ant for no reason,
or blow cigarette smoke into a cat's face,
or pull the legs off a ladybug
or kill a fly just because it's there—
all of which I have actually seen people do, like they don't even know it's cruel.

Kensington swats at the fly again, absently, still talking about my use of three-quarter view in the portrait.

"I'll get it," I cry, lurching forward. I grab one of the plastic cups the painting classes use for rinsing watercolor brushes and a thick piece of drawing paper.

"Gretchen, don't bother." Kensington.

"No, really, it'll only take a second."

"We're in the middle of your critique."

"I know, but let me catch it." It's flying around for a second and then it's on the corkboard. Not even moving. Almost like it knows that me catching it is better than being cooped up in this stuffy classroom forever, with Kensington swatting at it.

Cup over,
paper under,
there. Trapped.

"Will you open the window?" I ask.

"That was fast." Kensington pulls a key off her belt, unlocks the grate and opens the window.

Goodbye, fly.
Have some good buzzing out there.

"Are you finished now?" Kensington.

"I guess."

"Well, I'm happy to see you're making progress with your work, Gretchen. Let's move on."

That afternoon, Friday after gym, I'm standing with Katya in the hall outside the locker rooms. Our hair is still wet from the showers. School is out for the day, except for team practices.

"I have to take care of the monsters Saturday *and* Sunday," says Katya. "My mom has to cover someone's shift at the nursing home and my dad has some conference."

I don't want to be home alone all weekend.

"I could come down to Brighton Beach," I say. "We could cart them over to the aquarium."

"Oh. Um. Not with all three. It's too crazy. I'm gonna keep them at home or maybe just the playground." And she's right. With the three of them, we'd be outnumbered.

"What about tomorrow night?" I sound plaintive. "We could go to the movies. Or you could come sleep over. My folks are out of town."

"I can't. My mom is leaving for work at seven on Sunday."

Is she mad at me? She doesn't seem *mad at me. But she's blowing me off.*

I haven't even told her yet. There's never a good time to say to someone, "Hey, my parents are getting a divorce." And Katya's so into her family. The Belovs are family, family all the time.

The boys' locker room door swings open, and the Art Rats swarm into the hall. Titus, Shane, Adrian, Malachy and Brat. They're damp from the showers, geared up for the weekend. As they move past us, Shane bangs a locker hard, just to make noise, and I jump.

Why do boys do stuff like that?

"Friday, Friday, Friday!" Brat yells, his voice echoing down the hallway.

Adrian slams Brat in the back with a basketball, to shut him up, and Brat doubles over, his hands on his knees.

"I'm getting you for that!" cries Brat, turning red.

"Get me, get me, get me." Adrian spreads his arms wide.

"Shut up, losers." Titus.

"Didn't you see him hit me?"

"Just a tap, Tinker Bell," says Adrian. "Not hard."

Brat mutters to himself, and Malachy stops next to us, looking up and down in an exaggerated appraisal. "Girls, girls, girls!" Like he's pretending to be a pimp. "Ready for the weekend?"

"Ready as ever," says Katya.

Hell. Did someone just pinch my butt?
Someone did.
Shane. He's right behind me, laughing.
Why would he pinch my butt?
Why?
He's got a girlfriend. He barely even talks to me.

"Keep looking fine," says Malachy—then drops his pimp attitude in a fit of giggles. And then they are off down the hall, making noise about pizza and some movie they're going to catch at four o'clock.

"Hell," I mutter to Katya, digging around to find my subway pass in the crazy mess that is my backpack. "I do *not* understand what they are up to."

"Don't waste your energy," says Katya.

"Aren't they like alien beings?"

Katya puts on some lip gloss. "You think about them too much."

"What else is there to think about?"

"Drawing. Art. Literature. Politics. What to buy at the grocery store."

"Shane pinched my booty just now, did you catch that?"

Katya shakes her head. "What a schmuck."

"Do you think it meant something?"

"No."

"Why not?"

"Maybe he was asserting his male dominance," she concedes, "but it doesn't mean he has leftover feelings for you."

"What male dominance?"

"He's marking territory, like a dog," explains Katya. "Saying, see this butt? I can pinch it if I want. Gretchen won't do anything."

Now I feel like a half-wit, because I was actually flattered that Shane even noticed my booty enough to tempt his fingers in that direction. "Okay," I say. "But I don't think Shane is usually the booty-pinching type. He never pinched it before. Did he ever pinch yours?"

"I doubt it."

"Come on, Katya. Wouldn't you remember if Shane pinched your booty?"

"Okay, he never pinched it," she admits. "But I still don't think it means anything. He was male dominating. Or maybe flirting."

"But why is he flirting with me?"

"It's not the kind of flirting you want, anyway. Someone grabbing you from behind when he thinks he can cop a feel."

"Do you think he wants to be friends again?"

"No."

"Then is he manipulating me?"

"You think about it too much."

"How can there be flirting that doesn't mean anything?" I push.

"There just is." We're outside the school now, heading toward the subway. Katya lights a cigarette.

"Like you and Malachy?" I ask, feeling annoyed about the smoke and the no weekend plans.

"I wasn't flirting with Malachy."

I know I'm being a pain—but I can't help it.

My dad is a cheating, disappearing jerk and I love him like crazy;

Shane is a cold-fish-sometimes-flirty ex, and I can barely talk when he's in the room;

Titus is a sensitive guy one minute and sidekick to booty master Adrian the next.

If I can't figure out how to deal with the opposite sex, I'm going to lose my mind.

"Guys suck," I say to Katya. "Then they grow up to be men, and the men suck too."

"So forget them."

"Ha. That's like Spider-Man forgetting he's got Venom following him up a building."

Silence.

"Know what I wish?" I say. We are standing outside the subway now, before getting on our different trains.

"Hm." She seems distracted. "That you had a life?"

"Katya!"

"Okay. That Titus liked you."

"Besides that. Guess."

"Money? Beauty?"

"Besides those."

"Peace?"

"Besides that."

"Just tell me," sighs Katya. "What do you wish?"

"I wish I was a fly on the wall of the boys' locker room," I say.

I go home. The apartment is empty.

I watch TV. I read Kafka.

I order dumplings in hot oil and tofu with black bean sauce and eat as I flip through yesterday's newspaper.

I go to sleep.

part two

life as a vermin

Saturday morning, when I wake up, I am not in my bed.

I am not in my body, either.

I am standing, already, though I don't remember getting up, and I'm somewhere sunny.

It seems odd that I'm up before I'm awake, and odd that it's so bright in here, since I normally sleep with the shades down—but I only realize something is radically different when I stretch my arms,

and then my legs

and then my other legs.

Stupid hell, where are these legs coming from?

What, legs, what?

Where did I get extra legs?

They itch. I'll rub them together.

I must be dreaming still.

I wonder if the hot oil from last night is giving me weird dreams. I don't usually eat so much hot oil.

I'll probably wake all the way up in a minute, and stare at my messy room like usual, and pour a bowl of cereal and watch cartoons on TV and think about going running but not go, and try and call Katya and tell her what a strange dream I had.

Extra legs. I'm sure she'll have some Freudian analysis of the dream too. Like I have gherkin envy or something like that. Or I want to run away from something. Or stand up for something.

Whatever. I feel like stretching something else.

Hmm, ahh,

what is it I want to stretch?
Ah, yes, my wings,
my wings!
My WINGS.

I stretch them and it feels unbelievably great, these big, powerful, paper-thin wings coming from my shoulders. I have an incredible urge to flap them up and down rapidly. It's almost like they want to move on their own.

But I can't do that. I can't start flapping. It's too freakin' scary. Because this doesn't feel like a dream at all.

It feels absolutely realer than real. Realer than my regular life, even.

I open my eyes. Well, not exactly open them, because I don't have eyelids. It's more like turning them on, so I'm conscious not just of warm bright sunlight, but of the world around me. When I do, images are coming from everywhere, not only in front of me. I can see above, below, to the right, left and back of me—a full surround. But my brain has somehow adapted so that instead of being confused I'm able to look at a hundred different images and follow what's going on in each one.

In front of me is a window with frosted glass. I want to walk up it. The compulsion is strong, so despite my disorientation I get my six legs moving and—like Spider-Man—crawl up the glass to the top of the window.

Crawl up the glass!

When I reach the top, I stop and look around. In front of me is the ceiling, covered with good-smelling gray mildew spots. To my right, the side of the windowsill. Down to the back, showers and sinks. To my left, the other side of the windowsill and a row of toilet stalls with wooden doors painted a peeling blue. Directly behind me are rows of lockers and wooden benches. The tiles on the floor are dingy.

Where am I?

The room is familiar, and yet unfamiliar. A locker room. But not the one I'm used to. The tiles in the girls' room are white, and the walls are pink—but here are the same ancient, rusty showerheads, same square sinks. But bigger, with blue paint and blue tile.

And there are urinals.

Oh. My. God. I am in the boys' locker room.
The boys' locker room at Ma-Ha.

The girls' locker room is way smaller.

The boys have twelve showerheads and we have only six.

They have full-size lockers, and ours are only half-size.

And they have rows of minilockers, like mesh baskets that slide in and out of a large metal cabinet, with combination locks on them. For stuff they want to leave overnight.

The total unfairness pisses me off so much that for a minute I forget to think about how I've got wings,

and six legs,

and eyes that see out the back of my head.

I forget to wonder how any of this is happening or whether it's a dream.

I stand there on the window, rubbing my little forefeet together and fuming.

Why would theirs be bigger than ours?

We have to practically get dressed in the spray from the showers,

and shove our clothes into these tiny half-size lockers,

and why is it only the girls have to lug their gym shoes and shampoo in backpacks, when the boys have all this storage?

And why do they have nice long benches, when we have stubby ones?

And why do they have more showers, when everyone knows girls take longer showers than boys?

Ooh, they have a full-length mirror, too, and an extra tub for dirty towels, when ours is always overflowing.

Hell. I thought sexism was over already. I never thought it would be quietly living on in the architecture of my own school. We've been suffering in that tiny-ass locker room all this time, while the boys are showering in the lap of luxury.

Well, the paint is peeling and it's not exactly clean in here, but it's luxury compared to what the girls get.

Fuck.

Hell.

Every bad word out there.

I'm a fly. What does it matter what the locker rooms are like?

If I don't change back, I've got maybe a few weeks to live, if nobody swats me and no spider eats me. Pop will return from Hong Kong and I'll be gone without a trace. The apartment will be empty. No one will have seen me for eight days. Pop will call the police to make a missing person's report,

and Ma will come back and blame him for my disappearance,

and they'll be miserable and heartbroken and hate each other even more than they already do,

and all the while they're grieving and carrying on,

and the police are searching for my chopped-up shell of a body somewhere in a dark alley,

I'll just be buzzing hard up against this single window
unable to talk,
unable to explain,
unable to help or change back
or do anything—
stuck in a life even tinier than the one I left.
I might as well be dead.
And I will be soon enough.

I freak the hell out for several hours, just creeping up and down the windowsill with my heart in a knot of anxiety and fear.

But then, I think,

Hey, maybe I should try these wings.
They're here. On my back. I mean, I may be trapped in a nightmare, but I do have wings.
And that should mean I can fly, right?

I stretch them wide, then move them up and down. I bend my knees (all six) and

Flutter, flutter,
Flap
Bzzz bzzz bzzz
up!
UP!
I'm flying! I. Am. FLYING!
Ahhh,
whoa,
can't think and fly at the same time,
okay, don't think, fly,
up up,
now I've got it,
bzzzzzzzzzzzzzzzzz—
To the window on the other side!
Over the tops of the lockers!
Swoop down to the benches,
zip up to the lights,
buzz to the right,
to the left,
round in circles,
up,
up,
FLYING.
Wind in my face,

the sound of my own wings beating,
the feel of the air against them as they move,
the floor far below.

It's like riding downhill on a bike—a steep hill, so steep you wonder if it was a good idea to go down it, but you don't brake, you're not careful, you just go. Barely conscious of the houses whipping past you, barely conscious of your balance. All your attention on the pure sensation of movement.

Bzzzzzzzzzzzzzzzzz—

Stop.

Oh my god. I'm a superhero! It's like I've stepped right out of my own tiny life and into the Marvel Universe.

A superhero.

No longer am I Gretchen Yee,

trapped in that tiny life,

weighed down by stuff and divorce and boys and social weirdness and mean drawing teachers.

I am something different.

Something wondrous.

Something out of the ordinary.

Finally. Life is happening to me.

A superhero.

So: what should my name be?

Flyzina. (No. Too dumb.)

The Fly. (No, too literal.)

The Bug. (Too gross.)

Flyette. (Not bad, but too girly-girly.)

Flygirl. (Too obvious and probably too self-congratulatory, given the double meaning.)

The Buzz. (Also self-congratulatory, if you think like a buzz is a hot topic.)

I guess there's a reason superheroes rarely name themselves. They're usually given their titles by the news media or the adoring public, so they can be called stuff like Superman without having to say, "Yeah, I just looked in the mirror and thought, wow, I am just a super man, aren't I?"

What about:

Vermin. It's got a nice ring to it. But it sounds like a villain. There are a lot of villains named after bugs of some kind. Black Tarantula. Regular Tarantula. Scorpion. Beetle. Dragonfly. Spider-Wasp. Actually, wasn't there a Vermin in some of those old Spidey *and* Captain America *comics? And maybe in* Wolverine, *too. Vermin was a man turned into a cannibal humanoid rat by some evil experiment, and the wicked Zola used him as a tool to battle Spidey; then he went into psychotherapy to uncover his childhood abuse.*

Well, I'm obviously not him. I'll be the new Vermin. A good one. I've been warped by whatever changed me into this fly body—and now I'm going to use my superpowers for world salvation,

or citywide salvation,

or salvation of my parents' marriage,

and by extension for the permanent eradication of all

*weirdness and confusion between boys/men and girls/women
forevermore—*

*or if I'm not quite up to that, at the very least salvation of my
high school from all the poseur artist-types that make this place
such a living hell.*

*Cammie will be my nemesis. She's out there, talking about
stuff she read in ARTFORUM and turning boys into drooling idiots
with the power of her tremendous biscuits, and she must be neu-
tralized. Here comes Vermin to—*

*I could buzz in Cammie's ear, I guess, and track my dirty fly
feet across her art projects. I could find out stuff about her by
crawling in her backpack or coat pockets, or spy on her when she
doesn't know I'm looking. But that's not the stuff of action-
adventure comics. Marvel would never publish stories about a
goth-slut girl being annoyed by a housefly.*

Really, I can't do crap.

*I'm so tiny that anybody of normal size could defeat me with
a swatter or an aerosol can full of Fly-B-Gone.*

*The only thing I'm really likely to do is battle a mosquito for
domination of this stinky old locker room.*

*Now, if I could only figure out how to switch back and forth
at will, THEN maybe I could get something accomplished—find
out top-secret information and then use it for the good of all
humankind. (And insectkind, too, of course.)*

*Vermin. I could wear this great leather jumpsuit, and it
would zip up the front from crotch to turtleneck. Then I'd have big
shiny sunglasses that made me look the tiniest bit like a fly when*

I'm in human form. I'll retain some of my fly powers in my human body—like I'll be able to see things out the back of my head, and walk up walls—but to fly, or to sneak into secret places, or to appear to disappear and flummox my enemies, I'll turn into fly form. Just by snapping my fingers.

I spend a few minutes trying to snap my forelegs together to change back into a person.

It doesn't work. I get a snap going, but nothing happens when I do.

Then I try to *will* the change to happen.

No.

I try lying on my back and going to sleep like a person. I buzz back over to the windowsill and lie in the exact place where I first woke up, in case that makes any difference. I try a lot of little rituals—hopping up and down three times, twisting my head a funny way, kicking my legs out.

Nothing works.

I buzz over to one of the mirrors above the sinks, crawl up next to it and have a look at myself.

I am really, really ugly.

A monster. My body is dark gray with black stripes running along it and little wiry hairs sticking out all over, especially on my legs. My face is dominated by two giant composite eyes, and my lower lip is nothing but a tube.

It's hardly a face at all.

I can see now why people swat flies. They are insanely hor-rific looking.

I'll never get a boyfriend, looking like this.

Oh hell, that is the stupidest thing to think. I cannot believe I just thought that.

If I can't change myself back, then I'll be an insect forever, buzzing against the windowpane, living out my now-puny life ex-pectancy confined to a freakin' locker room.

I should be worried about that—not about whether this nasty-lookin' new body scorches my chances with Titus.

I am not a superhero at all. I am a garden-variety housefly.

Hell, I don't even have teeth.

Desperate to do something, anything, I try to get out of the locker room. I buzz over to the door and bang against the crack for a while (which hurts), then try to crawl under, but it's got one of those rubber sealers across it and there's no way to get through. Then I try the door that opens into the gymnasium, and I can smell the gym-smell of basketballs and dirty sneakers com-ing from the other side, but I can't get through that one either.

Maybe I can make a break for it when people come in for class on Monday, but there's nothing I can do at the moment. I'm stuck.

I buzz around in a flurry of anxiety, as if moving constantly will somehow burn off the panic that is welling inside of me.

Buzz
Buzz

Fuck
Fuck
What to do, what to do?
There is nothing to do.
ZZZZZZzzzzzzz
Can't get out
Can't change back
Can't get out
Can't change back

There's a spiderweb in one corner of the locker room, and in my panic I almost fly into it, veering back only at the last second and seeing the huge, hungry body of the spider sitting in the corner, eyeing me with silent fury as I zoom away.

Fuck. She could eat me.
Wrap me up in silk and suck my blood out.
Stay out of the corner
Stay out of the corner
Stuck
Stuck
Nothing to do
Nowhere to go
ZZZZZZzzzzzzz
ZZZZZZzzzzzzz

Jacked up with fear, I fly around the other side of the room in circles, my mind electric and unfocused. I go for hours upon hours, frantic, unconscious of anything except the desire to fly as fast as I can—as if I could fly myself farther from the spider, out of this room and out of my own fly-body.

Finally, after Saturday has faded into Sunday, which fades into night, I stop flying and go into a trance. Not exactly a sleep; more like my brain shutting off for a while, and my body going still out of complete exhaustion.

monday morning, I feel a bit better. Sunlight is streaming through the frosted glass, making pretty squares on the tile floor, and I quickly realize that what woke me up is the sound of a door swinging shut. The clock reads 7:40, twenty minutes before school starts.

A senior I know only by sight, this guy called Hugh, is in the room. He's African American, light skin, with short dreadlocks and a pair of supersize sunglasses always plastered on his face. I think he's in the sculpture program, and I know he used to go out with this girl Dawn.

Anyway, Hugh marches on in, bangs open a locker, tosses his leather bag on the floor, kicks off his sneakers and *drops his pants*.

He drops his pants!

How did I not think of this before?
I was so busy pretending to be a superhero,
and freaking the hell out about my situation
and hoping that any minute I'd be turned back,

that I never considered the obvious:
a locker room is for naked guys.
And when the school week starts, they're all going to come in here and take off their clothes.
It's happening now!
Naked guys!
Oh my god!

Hugh throws his pants into the locker. He's wearing little white undies on the bottom, a yellow T-shirt on top and argyle socks.

He takes off his shades and tucks them carefully into the bag, then pulls his shirt over his head. Then in nothing but his Calvins and socks, he pads over to the minilockers, unlocks his little drawer and pulls out some gym shorts and a pair of Nikes. He rummages in the leather bag for some sweat socks, a jock-strap and a gray T-shirt, then pulls down his underwear entirely.

Naked, except for argyle socks.

Now, this Hugh has an extremely fine body. He's a pretty coffee-with-milk color, and he's got a small waist and muscles rippling across his chest and back.

Seeing him naked, I feel a jolt of what I can only describe as lust.

I don't think I've felt lust before. Not like this.
If you'd asked me, I would have said I had—but now I think I hadn't.

Like with Shane: I was excited, I was into it and everything, and however far we went I was glad to go there—

but that was all in the context of us making out. I felt it when stuff got hot. Especially that time in the back of the movie theater. But I wasn't shot through with an urge to pounce on him when he was in the middle of doing something else. I didn't want to throw him on the tiles of the locker room,

and stick my tongue down his throat,
and run my hands across his chest,
and rip off my shirt.

But that's how I feel now, when Hugh gets naked.

It's like he's suddenly this lust object to me, not a person at all. And I'm now this person who can look at other people like objects—not objects to draw, but objects to have my way with.

Which is a new feeling.

But then I remember that I am not a human girl. And even if I were, Hugh would never look at me—probably doesn't even know who I am. He goes out with people like Dawn: tall confident girls with some junk in the trunk.

And besides, don't I actually find him an annoying poseur? Don't I actually think he's an airheaded slickster who doesn't care about anyone but his crew of tough seniors and the babes who follow them around? What am I doing lusting after someone I don't even think is a nice person?

Or is that the nature of lust? It's like an urge that disregards all the stuff that your brain knows you actually think.

I wonder if guys feel like this all the time. Or maybe if every-one feels like this all the time—everyone besides me—and that's why people act like such half-wits.

Anyway, although it sucks that I can't have my way with Hugh, at least I can buzz over and check out the goods in some detail.

Really, the only undressed man I've ever seen is my dad, and he stopped letting me in the bathroom with him about ten years ago. Since then, I've seen not one fully naked guy—although I have seen:

the movie *The Full Monty,* where you see a lot of guys in their underpants but never see the actual Monty itself, if you know what I mean,

several movies in which Ashton Kutcher or Josh Hartnett or some other star takes off his shirt,

lots of Greek and Roman sculptures with fig leaves covering their gherkins,

people at the beach, including one European guy whose bathing suit was so small it looked like nothing more than a little orange hammock for his package,

swimmers and divers on television, who are nice to look at but you can never look for long before they hurtle themselves into the water,

black-and-white illustrations in our biology textbook from last semester, which showed the gherkin circumcised and not, plus one of it being erect, which surprised me since I had figured it would stick out perpendicular to the body but really it turns out to point upward at like an eighty-degree angle,

and

Shane with his shirt off last fall, but nothing showing below the belt.

Oh, and we sometimes have models for drawing class, but because we're underage they always keep most of their clothes on.

I fly down to have a closer look at Hugh, who is taking off the argyles. I'm ashamed of myself, but I go in for close-up gherkin-information-gathering right away. I mean, I don't consider Hugh's privacy at all.

I'm a total Peeping Tom. Or Peeping Sally. Whatever.

Hm.

It's a blob of skin and hair.

It looks floppy and kind of humorous, actually.

You know how there are all these phallic symbols? Like giant skyscrapers and cannons and swords and things that are big and macho and shaped like a gherkin, supposedly, and they're symbols of masculine power?

Well, the actual gherkin doesn't look anything like a phallic symbol. Honestly, the idea that Spider-Man and Orlando Bloom and the president of the United States all have these blobs of skin and hair flopping off their midsections underneath their clothes and bouncing around when they walk—it's actually funny. Worse than biscuits; those bounce a bit when I run but it's

really not a problem. Honestly, if I had what Hugh has got be-
tween my legs, I don't know how I'd ever even sit down or pull on
a pair of pants, much less play dodgeball.

It's a major liability.

I think he's medium-size, though I don't have anything to
compare it to. It's floppy and even shrively-looking. Like in this
state, at least, none of those words people use seems to fit.

My sword,
my torpedo,
my pink trombone,
my rocket,
my Longfellow,
my voodoo stick,
my staff of life.

It's nothing like what you'd think when guys are bragging
about being well hung, or sticking it in some girl, or some crap
like that. I mean, it's got a kind of magnetism about it, like it's
ugly and good-looking at the same time.

But not what I had imagined.

It's more human, I guess.

Hugh swats at me vaguely as I buzz around his midsection. I
fly up to the top of the lockers and keep staring at him.

It is interesting to see a boy's body up close. My own body
has a thousand imperfections; I mean, my human body did,
when I had one. Fuzzy-looking eyebrows, no muscle definition,
thickish ankles, bitten fingernails—but I never gave any thought
to the idea that a popular guy like Hugh would have imperfec-

tions, too. I mean, overall he has a great physique. Girls look at him all the time. But he's got a spray of zits across his shoulders,

and his belly hangs over his waistband when he bends over,

and his butt has curly black hairs on it, like they didn't know they were supposed to stop at the top of his legs,

and one of his nipples is pierced, which is not my thing, but I guess he must like it,

and his feet are bony and have hairy knuckles,

and his skin looks dry in patches, here and there,

and his legs are kind of thin in proportion to his top half. None of the Greek statues ever has legs like that.

So it's like I simultaneously have this lust thing going on and this objective evaluation of his flaws.

You wouldn't think you could do both at the same time, but you can. I can.

I must still be at least partly human, or he wouldn't make me hot and bothered the way he does.

Hugh is nearly dressed and the clock reads 7:50 when the door slams open again and I can hear shouts in the hallway and a horde of senior boys comes into the locker room and starts changing clothes for gym class. Some of them are groggy and carry paper cups of coffee from the deli across the street from school, or cans of Coke. Others are boisterous, socking each other on the arms. They invade the space, throwing off their jackets, dropping their pants, whizzing through the combinations on their minilockers.

The boys are wearing boxers and briefs; they're skinny and fat; they're black, white, Latin, Asian. They're all seniors, so some are hairy in all kinds of ways I hadn't really imagined; hairy like the men I see on the beach at Coney Island—some with hair that goes across their collarbones, some with a big stripe of hair down the middle of their abdomens, some with hair on their lower backs, or on the backs of their upper arms. One guy has nipples that poof out a bit in a girly way. Another guy, a quiet boy who everyone knows already had an exhibition of his paintings at a downtown gallery, has a surgery scar across his stomach. A third has a series of tiny white scars crisscrossing his forearms. I think he must have made them himself, with a razor.

They're being macho, most of them, trading insults and laughing loudly. A number of them pee in the urinals. At first it's overwhelming, this stampede of half-naked half-manhood, but they're not all as fine as Hugh, so pretty soon I get ahold of myself and buzz down to inspect more gherkins.

Some are quite pink, while others are surprisingly brown, and it doesn't seem to follow directly from the skin color on the rest of the guy's body. And lots of boys are circumcised—but not everybody. I saw two that still had the foreskin attached, looking like the drawings in the biology textbook.

Also, I had always thought of the gherkin part as the main event, but if you see one that's peeing, or hanging around not doing anything, it's only part of a larger package. By which I mean, the balls are there—and they're nearly as big as the actual gherkin.

This, too: when you see men's booties in the movies, I think they must be waxing because so many of these boys have hair back there or roundabout.

None of the guys checks each other out in the goods department. When they are peeing they all stare straight ahead like there's something fascinating on the wall.

Eventually, there's no more information to be gathered and the guys are mainly in their sweats and shorts anyway, and I hear Sanchez blow his whistle, sharp from the other side of the gymnasium double doors.

The boys slam their lockers and run into the gym. I try to follow them, but the doors are swinging, and I can't time it right, and when I'm flying I don't seem to have a whole lot of precision. I mean, I can go in a general direction but I can't steer exactly through a door above someone's head at just the right second.

I also try landing on a particular person and riding through the doors on him, but the first guy bats me off, and the second one, though he doesn't notice me at all, dislodges me as soon as he starts moving. My legs aren't strong enough to hold on to a moving object like that, and I'm compelled to let go of his sweatshirt. I try again anyhow, but the third one tries to kill me, slamming his hand hard onto his own arm—and I barely escape.

I fly back to my perch on the window and sit there for forty-five minutes by the locker room clock, listening to what sounds like basketball practice in the gym. Then the seniors troop back in and shower.

The whole shower scene is funny. A few of them are quiet, like I am when I have to shower in public, scooting in and out of the water as fast as they can and wrapping themselves quickly in

89

towels. But a lot of them are horsing around, throwing soap at each other and laughing, having conversations, being rowdy.

The girls never do that.

The bell rings, and the few remaining seniors throw on their clothes and run out. Then a swarm of freshmen come in.

It's the same drill—only, compared to the seniors they look like little boys. They're smaller, slighter, less hairy. Their voices haven't all changed, and the din they make sounds more like playground noise than manly banter.

Then third period is African dance elective. Only two boys come in.

I don't know either of them, and they're shrimpy and scrawny—but African dance is just for juniors and seniors, so they must be at least sixteen. They're probably geeks, since even in artsy Ma-Ha, dance class is only taken by boys who are so far down the social totem pole that they might as well take it if they feel like it. Everyone will think they're losers for taking dance—but everyone already thinks that anyway.

One boy is Latino, with short hair shaved up the sides. He's not more than five foot three, and he's wearing a new-looking orange pocket T-shirt that no doubt his mama bought him, and jeans that hang too high on his hips.

The other boy is only slightly taller, but gangly like a puppy. He's African American, with tight braids across his skull, black Clark Kent glasses and a shirt that reads UP YOURS. They change into sweatpants, leaving their feet bare.

Orange: "You see G this morning?"

Up Yours: "Nah."

Orange: "Me neither. I actually waited for her out on the steps."

Up Yours laughs. "You're gone, boy."

Orange: "Whaddya think she's drawing all the time?"

Up Yours: "How should I know?"

Orange: "She's so intense."

Up Yours: "You should talk to her. You can't be going on like this forever. She was sitting alone in the lunchroom, I saw her last week."

Orange: "Yeah, but she *likes* it that way." He makes what is meant to be a glamour face: "I vant to be aloooone." He reverts to normal. "She's not like a regular girl where you can ask if she wants potato chips. She'd like, bite my head off."

Up Yours: "Whatever. But you're gone. You gotta do something about it or switch over to some other girl."

The boy in orange doesn't answer this; he's rooting around in his backpack for a combination lock.

Up Yours continues: "But she is hot. I give you that. Even I noticed she looked smokin' on Friday."

Orange: "That tiny tank top? She was workin' that milkshake."

Up Yours: "Red shirt like her hair."

They are talking about me.
About me.
I think.
I mean, G is for Gretchen. And I've got red hair. And I sit alone in the lunchroom. And I draw sitting on the steps in the morning.

And I wore a red camisole shirt on Friday, when it was so warm. I can wear them easily 'cause I've got almost nothing on top, so it doesn't matter.

Except maybe it does. At least, these guys were looking. And seeing something.

A milkshake.

I never think people are looking at me. Are people looking at me?

The boy in orange thought I was working the milkshake.

Could I be working it and not even know I'm working it? Have I got anything to work?

I've never even seen these guys before. Never even seen them, and they know who I am and where I like to sit, and what I was wearing last Friday. Like they've got crushes on me, or one of them does. "You see G this morning?"

Someone has a crush on me. Short Orange with the geek pants.

I never thought anyone would have a crush on me. I never thought anyone would like me more than I liked him.

I mean, I don't exist, not next to girls like Cammie and Taffy. I'm the girl who doesn't exist to other people.

The boys head off for class, and I listen to the sound of drumbeats coming from the gym. Afterward, as Orange and Up Yours are standing by their lockers, some of the junior boys start to trickle in for fourth period. And for no reason that I can tell, this guy named Gunther thwaps Up Yours on the butt with a towel. He has a thuggy-looking nose. "How's the dancing lesson, ladies?" he asks.

"Fine," mutters Orange, pulling off his T-shirt and throwing on a clean one without even taking a shower. (The new shirt is also orange, but an older, softer-looking one with ORANGE CRUSH written across the back.)

"Wanna show me some moves?" asks Gunther. "Some twirly twirls?"

"No thanks," whispers Orange, like he's been invited to drink tea.

"It's African dance, you tool," says Up Yours. "It's not some ballet crap." He splashes water on his face at the sink, but doesn't shower either. Like the two of them are trying to get out of there before the situation gets any worse.

"Aw, just one little twirly, Tinker Bell," teases Gunther. "I'm not asking for much. Why are you giving me such a hard time?"

"It's called a contraction, the move we mainly do," says Orange, quietly. "Not a twirly. You contract your abdomen, like from the center of your body."

"Carlo, don't explain him anything," says Up Yours, taking his glasses out of his locker. "He doesn't want to know."

"Oh, I'm very interested!" sneers Gunther. "A contraction: is that like in childbirth?" He's bigger than they are, looming over.

"Not like that," says Carlo (Orange).

"You *would* be doing contractions, you ladies."

"Just fuck off!" yells Up Yours, losing his crap. "Why can't you leave us alone?"

BANG. Gunther slams him into a locker. "You telling me to fuck off, you Mary Poppins faggot little smart-mouth?"

"Ow!"

"Is that what I heard you saying? That I should *fuck off*?"

"You heard me."

"Tell me your name, fag."

"Don't touch me."

"What's your name, you little ballet dancer?"

Up Yours is silent. Gunther grabs his ear and twists it, hard. "I said, what's your name?"

He squeaks it out. "Xavier, okay? Xavier."

"Xavier what?"

Nothing.

"I said, Xavier *what*?"

"Xavier Briggs."

"Well, Miss Xavier Briggs," growls Gunther, "repeat after me. I am a . . ."

"I am a . . ." Xavier is trembling as Gunther leans over him.

". . . ballet-dancing faggot."

". . . ballet-dancing faggot," Xavier repeats.

"Now mind your step, Mary Poppins," says Gunther, straightening up. "You're being watched from now on. You understand?"

Xavier (Up Yours) swallows hard. "Yeah." He squirms from under the heavy paw Gunther has placed on his shoulder, and as soon as he's free, he and Carlo grab their packs and run for the door.

They're gone.

I buzz down and circle Gunther's head, just because I want to do something, anything. But he claps his hands so quickly he almost squashes me between them, and I zip back up to the top of the lockers before he can try it again.

So much for my superpowers.

It's not long before I'm distracted from thinking about Carlo and Xavier's persecution. A major wave of junior boys rushes into the locker room, yelling and stripping off their clothes. Two of them are tossing a ball around, shirtless. Another isn't wearing any underwear when he pulls down his shorts.

Some of these boys are really fine.

That guy in the red boxers has a great booty. Round and hard like a ball. Like it's begging someone to squeeze it.

Ooh, and this guy over here with the mohawk. He's, um . . . well endowed. You'd never know to look at him—thin and dressed in black, with a lot of piercings. Dyed blue hair and blue eyes. Not a standout physical specimen just walking down the hallway, but without his clothes he's . . .

One thing is for sure. When I turn back—if I ever do—I'm definitely going to try and get me some sex.

I mean, not too much, not sex sex, not more than I'm ready for, but I'd be all over rubbing my Gretchen Yee body up against some man-flesh, if you know what I mean. Somewhere dark with candles all around. Or somewhere brightly lit and dangerous, like a locker room floor.

It's funny, I had no idea I was this kind of person. I mean, I thought I was all for romance, and that I wanted secret love notes

*and hand-holding, and good-night kisses on the street corner by
my apartment, under an awning on a rainy night.*

*And I do want all those things. It's not like I've stopped
wanting them.*

It's just that now I've got urges.

Like I can't stop thinking about it.

*Like I know what a guy means when he says he's got a one-
track mind.*

Fourth period is juniors, fifth is seniors and juniors mixed,
sixth is sophomores, seventh is freshmen again. The Art Rats
won't show up until eighth.

As the hours pass, I entertain myself by making a mental
classification chart for the male booty. Now, someone could well
accuse me of objectifying the opposite sex. But really, all these
boys are shampooing and rinsing and toweling off, and some of
them are even strutting about in the altogether like roosters.
What else is a girl to do? Think about literature?

Please.

So here's my chart.

The A-plus booty is slightly rounder than you'd expect from
the rest of the boy it's attached to. It's the superhero, Greek-
statue butt, with a slightly melonish quality that makes you want
to thump it. It's also free of hair and pimples (you'd be surprised
how many guys have zits on their booties. It's quite shocking).

The grade-A butt is a surprising step away from the A-plus
variety. It's tiny and narrow. There's no way you could ever mis-
take it for a girl's. It would be ideal if this particular butt was

paler than the rest of the boy—if he's got a bit of a tan. But it's only April, so no luck.

Only jocks have the A-minus kind—of which there are very few at Ma-Ha, since everyone's an artiste. But the few guys who are muscled and built have these vulnerable little booties. It's touching. Like the rest of the body is macho macho, and then there's this soft squishy butt that says, "Hey, I'm a person like anyone else."

The B-plus is quite common: rather flat on top, and soft-looking, but makes a nice pair of semicircles when it meets the legs.

B: the plump boy's booty. There are quite a number of chubby boys at Ma-Ha, and there is a real advantage to having some extra padding in the downstairs department. They've got these juicy round booties that look like quite a handful.

B-minus goes to the common B-plus variety, only hairy. Alternately, with pimples.

The C-grade booties I lump together. A couple of stretch marks don't bother me—even some of the A-plus boys have them—but a few of these guys have a whole map of tiny white scars; or they're really, really hairy; or they're lumpy-looking. Others are flat and saggy, or covered with mysterious-looking rashes.

One junior with a definitely C-minus butt had a gorgeous face—all beautiful dark eyes and high cheekbones.

The Ds—well, what teacher gives Ds? It's just unkind. And I only see one that I would give a failing mark. It's like the bottom of a wild boar—flat and saggy and pimply and hairy all at once.

And the moral is: you never know what's going on underneath someone's pants until you see it for yourself.

Seventh period ends and the freshmen filter out. First of the Art Rats to come in is Titus.

Oh my god, I hadn't thought about this,
there's been so much going on,
but I'm about to see Titus naked.
Naked!

Suddenly, all my spying seems wrong.

I mean, it's one thing to check out people you don't speak to,
who don't even know you exist,
but it's another thing to spy on people you see every day in
class. People you know.
Should I look at Titus?
I'd be furious if he (or anyone else) were watching me *in the*
locker room.
But I can't shut my eyes. Literally, I can't. I've got no eyelids.
And I've got eyes in the back of my head, so I can't look away. No
matter where I fly in the locker room, I can see Titus as he heads
toward his locker.
Besides, I want to see.

I know it's wrong, but the boy I think about all the time is taking off his clothes in front of me.

Would anyone in my position honestly look away?

Once he bangs open his locker, Titus throws his backpack on the floor. He tears off his jacket and T-shirt, then puts on his gym sweatshirt right away.

Like he's embarrassed. Even though he's alone.

I catch a glimpse of a very, very thin torso—soft white skin on the sides of his body, no hair anywhere much—and then it's gone. He yanks down his pants and his boxers with his face practically inside his open locker, and I can see his booty is a solid A—the small, narrow kind. His legs are thin as well. Spindly, you could even say.

He pulls a pair of white briefs out of the bag and puts them on quickly, followed by baggy gray gym shorts. His pale calves look out of place beneath the wide legs of the shorts.

He sits down on the bench, as if relieved, and slowly pulls on a pair of sweat socks. Then he goes over to his minilocker and gets his running shoes.

Adrian and Malachy bang in, along with a couple of sophomore boys from the photography department, guys I recognize from classes, but whom I don't know. Brat trails in after them, lugging his oversize book bag.

"Hey," they say to Titus.

"Hey," he says back.

"Crap," mutters Adrian, running his hand through his spiky

hair. "Can you believe what that faggot Meadows gave us for lab homework? We don't even get the weekend to do it." He's changing his clothes, and his body looks both energetic and relaxed, like he's comfortable in his skin.

"Whatever," Titus says, "I don't think he's gay."

"Well, he's sure a bastard," says Adrian. "You give me that?" He pulls on a T-shirt and grabs his shoes from his minilocker.

"Yeah," laughs Titus. "I give you that."

"I hope we don't have dodgeball again," pipes up Brat with a nervous laugh. "When did Sanchez say we were gonna do the hockey unit?"

No one answers him. It's like he didn't even say anything.

"Come on, Ip," says Titus. Adrian shoves his feet into his sneakers and the two of them slam through the doors that lead to the gymnasium.

Brat tries again as Shane comes in. "Hey, Shane, what's up?"

Shane grunts, he's running late, and starts pulling off his clothes. Brat, already dressed for class, bends down and rummages through his pack as if looking for something.

Shane looks great without his shirt. I remember from our earlier, um, encounters. He plays pickup basketball every weekend. He's white, tall and blond, with strong-looking legs and visible muscles across his abdomen. A small birthmark on his neck, strawberry-colored. He tugs his sweats down over his sneakers and pulls his shorts on over his gray Calvin Klein briefs; then he puts on a white T-shirt and heads into the gym. Now it's just

Malachy and Brat left, Brat still rummaging in that pack as if he's doing something important.

I've been so busy checking out Shane that I missed seeing Malachy naked. In his gym clothes, he looks incongruous, as he always does. The quadruple-pierced ears, the thick black wristbands, the black socks. He doesn't look like an athlete, though he's actually not bad at sports.

"Hey, hey," Brat says, after a minute.

"Brat." Malachy looks up. "What's going on?"

"Not much," says Brat. He stops the pretense of rummaging and shoves the pack into his locker. "If we're doing the hockey unit, you wanna be partners?"

In gym, we have to find partners for practicing things, like kicking a soccer ball back and forth, or hitting a hockey puck. I always pick Katya, and she always picks me. Titus is usually with Adrian, Shane is usually with Malachy, and Brat—I can't think who he's usually with. Maybe he switches around.

"Yeah, okay," says Malachy, and the two of them head into class.

The locker room is empty for forty-five minutes, and I can hear the pucks hitting the walls of the gym, and the scrape of the wooden sticks on the floor. Then they troop back in.

Sanchez enters and blows a whistle. He's done this every hour after class, except for third-period African dance, when he probably takes a coffee break. "Hit the showers! Now! I don't wanna hear your whining!"

In the girls' locker room, we get the same drill from

Kobayashi, the assistant teacher. We have fewer showerheads, though, so she lines us up and stands over us, yelling, "Use the soap, ladies!" and "Speed it up, people are waiting!" until most of us are through.

The boys don't line up; they just mill around, so Sanchez can't keep good track of who's showering and who's not. But most of them crush toward the showers, towels around their waists, and rinse off. Shane is drenched in sweat and heads straight for the water, dropping his clothes on the floor. He showers efficiently and washes his hair. Adrian joins him quickly, leaning his hands up against the tile wall as if he's tired and letting the water run down his back. Eventually, Sanchez heads back into the gym to get ready for whatever he does next, and the last remaining boys either skip showering or horse around in there, pushing each other's wet shoulders and talking about hockey.

Titus has got a big bruise on his knee, like he fell down or got hit with a hockey puck. He's one of the last guys in, and he showers so fast it's like he's got it down to a science. Soap in all the most important areas, rinse front, rinse back, over and out. Before he's even back to his locker he's got his regular T-shirt back over his head, not even drying his skin, and he puts his underwear on underneath his towel.

Once he's dressed, he transforms back into the Titus I'm used to seeing. Confident, relaxed, thoughtful. The nervous, underweight kid with the hunted look has disappeared.

"You still want to see that movie?" he asks the guys. "I called Moviefone. It's five-fifteen at Second and Eleventh."

"I'm there," says Shane.

"I would," says Adrian, pulling his jeans on. "But I'm broke. They don't pay crap at the hardware store. Can't we rent something and go to your house?"

"No." Titus sounds decisive.

"Why not? Your dad's gotta be at work."

"Yeah," Titus concedes. "But—"

"And you're only like five blocks away. If we go to mine or Shane's we have to go all the way into Queens."

"That's cool," says Shane. "Let's go to Titus's."

"Not happening," says Titus.

"Come on," chimes in Malachy. "Brat's in Brooklyn, and we could go to mine, but my mom'll be home. And you know how she is."

"Plus it's small as crap," laughs Shane.

"Exactly," says Malachy, ruefully. "Whaddya say, Titus?"

"He's got TiVo," Shane adds. "He told me. And his dad's some big-money doctor, so you know he's got like a big leather couch and probably a fridge full of food. Come on, Titus. We promise we won't trash anything."

"Yeah, right," says Titus. "You guys are like a hurricane."

"We'll behave, I swear," says Adrian. "Come on, your pops will never know the difference. Don't make me go home, now."

"That's not it, anyway," says Titus.

"We'll even vacuum," says Adrian, getting down on his knees in mock supplication. "Brat will vacuum."

"Me?" whines Brat. "Why me?"

"I'll dust, Malachy will pick the chips out of the couch and Shane will sweep the floor," continues Adrian, laughing but half serious. "You can't argue with that."

"Yes, I can," says Titus. "Let's go to Luigi's." (The pizza place around the corner.)

"Crap," says Adrian, standing up. "I told you I don't have cash."

"I'll spot you," says Titus. "But just Ip, not you other bottom-feeders."

"But—"

"We're *not* going to my house," says Titus. "End of discussion."

He slings his pack over his shoulder and bangs out the door. The rest of them follow.

I wish I had a crew I could hang around with after school like that. I mean, I've kind of got Katya, but only kind of. And no one else. The Art Rats just assume they're hanging out together— they don't have to ask in advance. They're friends; and friends do stuff together.

But on another note—

why won't Titus let them in his house?

It sounds like he's got money. I mean, it's New York City and funds are tight everywhere. Some kids are rammed into tiny apartments with big families, or their places are sorry-ass and they feel weird about playing host. This I can understand. But Shane said Titus is living pretty large,

and if he's only five blocks away, he's in a posh neighbor-

hood. Of course, even with money people's parents can still be
nightmares:

> *they can yell,*
> *or be drunk,*
> *or hover around like everyone's business is their business—*
> *but Titus admitted that his dad's not gonna be home. And*
> *I'm pretty sure his mom lives out West somewhere.*

> *So what's the problem? Why would Titus pay for Adrian's*
> *pizza just to avoid people coming over?*

After eighth period, some guys trickle in for basketball—
mainly seniors. The track and field boys come in, too, before they
head to the park for practice.

When they clear out, I'm left alone as the light from the
window dims, and I fall still and let my thoughts run.

> *Why has this happened to me?*
> *If it's merely a cosmic accident, or some strange allergic re-*
> *action to the celery soda, or exposure to nuclear waste or some-*
> *thing else highly toxic (like whatever I stepped in Friday morning,*
> *that gel-like grossness), then nothing's ever going to change me*
> *back.*

> *I'm a fly for life. This is my world now. I might as well*
> *accept it.*

> *But I don't. Accept it. It's too horrible. I have to change back.*
> *A different possibility:*
> *Some power—some magic beyond my control—has done*
> *this to me.*

God.

In which case, God is punishing me. But for what, precisely?

Being too lame to clean my room?

Too shy to talk to the boys I like?

Too obsessed with superheroes?

Angry at my dad?

I mean, I am a schmuck in all these ways and more, and I also say "hell" too much, but if God has decided that I deserve possibly eternal insectitude for what I've done, then what is he (or she) doing to all the rapists and murderers?

Maybe the sinners of the world get turned into some kind of vermin when they die, and the worse you are, the worse kind of vermin you become. Houseflies are regular people who swore and never did their homework. Rats are the people who shoplifted or cheated on their spouses. And the cockroaches are all unrepentant killers.

But are we then forced to live as vermin for all eternity? Or do we die again at the end of our pitiful, horror-filled vermin lives and then go on to burning in flames or lying on the rack or whatever Hell is, the way we usually think of it?

And if this is Hell, then why does eternal damnation look exactly like the boys' locker room at Ma-Ha? And why am I being punished for my short, schmucky life by watching naked boys parade around the showers?

And is my human body actually lying dead in my bed because of some strange latent disease that killed me in the middle of the night, *or because the ceiling fell in,*

or because a serial killer jimmied the lock, crept into my bedroom and chopped my body into bits? If so, then my corpse is rotting and decaying and smelling up the apartment, since no one is even going to check on me until Saturday when Pop gets home from Hong Kong.

Then he'll find my dead body,

and everyone will be sorry,

and Katya will be sad she didn't return my messages,

and Kensington will feel guilty about how she treated me in front of everyone,

and Titus will realize he loved me passionately,

and so will Shane for that matter.

Which would be kind of nice. But not too likely.

Hm. What else could it be?

The fly I rescued. It was magic somehow, and did this to me as a reward for rescuing it from Kensington. Maybe it thought I'd be happier being a fly than being a human being. Because obviously, I wasn't a happy girl.

Even so, even an insect could be expected to realize that human beings generally like to remain human beings. We want to eat Chinese food and rule the planet and have sex with others of our species. If that fly made me into a fly so as to give me a happier life, I'd think it would have made me a total fly— interested in mating with other flies, wanting to lay eggs in poo, and not thinking all these human thoughts and lusting after high school boys.

So what if it was that old man on the train? "You think you'll be like this forever," he said, "but you'll change before you know it."

It seemed like he was talking about aging, how he couldn't go ice dancing anymore, and could barely even stand up by himself. I thought he was saying, "Hey, enjoy your youth today because it's not going to last forever. Don't waste it feeling sorry for yourself when your legs still work and you don't have heart fibrillations."

But maybe he was saying,

"Hey, enjoy your youth today because I'm putting a curse on you and TURNING YOU INTO AN INSECT FOR THE REST OF YOUR LIFE, STARTING TOMORROW."

Though really, he was too nice to do that. Maybe instead it was "Hey, you don't appreciate your life enough, you nice young thing, so I'm going to teach you how good you've got it by turning you into a fly." In which case, he'd only do it for like a few days.

But again, same question. Why would a gnome-fairy pick the locker room? Nothing like this ever happens in Lord of the Rings or Harry Potter. No one waves a magic wand and says: "Thou shalt spy on naked boys for eight hours a day and learn all the mysteries of the gherkin."

And why a fly? Wouldn't he pick the body of an old woman so I could learn to appreciate youth, or do a body swap with me like in Freaky Friday, *where the mom becomes the girl and the girl becomes the mom?*

Which would mean I'd be him—

Ooh, unless he's just so freakin' old that he's lost all powers except turning people into flies. Like he wants to turn them into other people, or birds, or horses, but his magical zapper is so weak and his confabulator is so muddled that whatever he's trying to do turns out a housefly.

But that's a little far-fetched, isn't it?

Think, Gretchen. Be practical.

Why would I be a fly?

Why would I be here?

It can really only be one thing. I must have turned into a fly on the wall of the boys' locker room because I wished that very particular thing, out loud.

And the only person who heard me wish it was Katya.

So Katya—what? Turns out to have magical powers?

Okay, even if I go with this idea, that my best friend is some sorceress and can turn people into animals, I don't think she'd have thought I was serious when I wished to be a fly.

It was a stupid METAPHOR. Fly on the wall of the locker room. Like so I could see what went on inside, without anyone knowing I was there.

I wasn't saying I actually wanted to live in the body of a freakin' vermin.

Nothing makes any sense.

Exhausted, I go into a daze and veg out for the rest of the night—until the slam of Hugh's locker wakes me up just in time for a nice Tuesday-morning view of his A-plus booty.

At first, I'm psyched to spend the morning looking at naked

guys—and I do gather some more information. Like the student body president wears tight black underwear. And there are guys who pluck their eyebrows. And if left alone half-naked in front of a mirror, even for a second, a surprising number of guys will start flexing. And others will dance.

But after first and second period, I lose interest in the whole voyeur thing. I've seen it all before. Me! Who yesterday morning had never before seen a naked man unrelated to me (and that was ten years ago anyway) has now seen the private equipment of an estimated 110 boys, if you figure I get a decent look at ten guys per class, and eight class periods every day, plus after-school sports and two classes this morning.

I've seen them pee, I've seen them waggle, I've even seen them hanging out with—shall I say—a certain degree of enthusiasm.

Boys' bodies used to seem alien and intimidating. I thought they'd all look like they do in the movies (smooth, muscular, hairless), except they might also look horrible and gross down in the gherkin department, which was a place I was not even thinking about because it seemed too overwhelming.

And now—it's all different. They're just bodies. They're just people.

third period, after class. Gunther with the thuggish nose gives my little African dance boys a hard time again. "Hey, Tinker Bells, show us your splits. You can do the splits, can't you? Let's see what you got."

No answer.

"Aw, don't be modest, ladies."

No answer again, but Xavier (Up Yours) mutters something low under his breath and instantly Gunther turns mean, whomping his backpack into Xavier's arm on purpose.

"What was that for?"

"I told you, don't start with him." Carlo (Orange) grabs his friend's elbow and heads for the door. "Ignore it."

"No, what was that *for*?" Xavier persists.

Gunther bangs a locker, making a huge hollow-metal noise. "To remind you to shut yourself up, Mary Poppins," he growls. "Don't go messing with me or you'll never do your faggot contractions again."

"You calling me a faggot?"

"Yes. I am calling. You. A. Faggot."

"Bite me!" mutters Xavier. He's about to say more, but Gunther's fingers have tightened into a fist, and Carlo grabs Xavier's arm hard and drags his friend away, out into the hall where it's safe.

When they're gone, it's quiet.

Gunther turns and gets changed.

Like nothing happened.

He says hi to some guys coming in for class, laughs with some people, talks about something on TV, talks about the end-of-April sculpture course exhibit. He seems like an okay guy.

You'd never know he'd just been torturing a pair of dance geeks like it was an Olympic sport he was trying to medal in.

fifth period is juniors and seniors again, then sophomores sixth and freshmen seventh. I get bored, so I buzz over to the mini-lockers and peek inside them. They're mesh baskets with combo locks, labeled with last names. I can sit on the edge of each one and look down to see the contents.

It's rather disappointing, actually. If we had them, the girls' minilockers would be full of shampoo and conditioner and deodorant and moisturizer and makeup, plus extra socks and water bottles. You could tell so much about a girl from what was in her minilocker. Mine would have this great rose-scented lip gloss that you can also use as a moisturizer or to get your bangs to go over to the side, because it's really just nice-smelling Vaseline. Plus this conditioner I bought in Chinatown that's good for Asian hair that I've tried bringing in my bag, only the top comes loose and it leaks all over. Katya's would have this purple gel soap I know she's crazy about, and a gray eye pencil and her perfume that smells like aloe vera.

But hardly any of the boys have that kind of stuff. There are a few things of deodorant, and a couple jars of hair gel. Otherwise, most of them have sneakers and nothing else.

They don't even need these lockers. It's so unfair.

Titus's minilocker has a pair of New Balance sneakers and some deodorant that says COOL WAVE. I crawl up and smell it. Gross, I know, but I do. It has an ocean scent. Shane's has two pairs of sneakers—one that looks like it's for basketball, the other for running. Adrian's has a knee brace that I've sometimes seen him wearing. Only Brat's is really interesting. It's absolutely packed with stuff, and doesn't even have any sneakers in it at all. It looks like he shoves things in there from his backpack, maybe that he doesn't want to carry around or put into his hall locker for some reason. There's a pile of magazine clippings, held together with a paper clip. I can't see the rest of them, but the top one is a picture of a girl wearing red lipstick, so dark it's almost black. There are four small notepads, all covered with scribbly handwriting—lists of stuff to do, diary entries, phone numbers. The top page of one reads "eggs 4 mom, electric toothbrush, zit stuff, nail clipper." A list of things to buy before he goes home. The top page of another, also a list, reads

Ip—a schmuck. Sometimes. Too much of the time.
Titus—slick.
Malachy—a listener.
Shane—repressed. But what?
Cammie—babe.
Taffy—cipher.
Katya—nice. To everyone.
Gretchen—?? An enigma.
Kensington—a bitch.

There are doodles around the edge. I can't read anything on the other notebooks or pages.

There's also a pack of cigarettes and three worn-looking packs of matches, a tube of anti-itch cream, a tube of Blistex, a thing of little round stickers with puppies on them, a blue plastic egg that looks like it has a toy inside, a key chain with a silly-looking rabbit on it and no keys, some baseball cards, a couple of charcoal pencils, a bunch of Post-it notes and a Bean Curd Baby in a small, clear plastic box. A Bean Curd Baby!

I love those things.

the bell rings after seventh and the Art Rats trickle in as the freshmen swarm out. As the door to the hallway swings, I catch a glimpse of Shane pushed up against the brick wall by Jazmin LeMaitre, his girlfriend.

His hand is on her butt and she's licking his neck.

Not like I haven't seen it a million times. The two of them are very PDA. But it gives me a sick feeling anyway. Like, why does Jazmin have everything so effortlessly? Sophistication, talent, Shane. She wants something, she goes after it and gets it. She's always wearing some interesting combination of clothes *and* her photographs hung in the citywide exhibition *and* she's got a boyfriend who's devoted to her.

She wants it, she takes it.

Why can't I?

Titus has his shirt off now. I can't think about anything else.

Titus
Titus
Titus

Before he can pull on his gym sweatshirt, Adrian grabs one of Titus's sneakers and tosses it up on top of a locker.

"Ip, you madman!" yells Titus. He reaches up, trying to reach the top of the locker, and I can see the narrow muscles of his back ripple; his left shoulder blade sticks out sharply.

I want to draw him so bad. To capture what I see.

But the moment is gone,

and I can't draw him because I'm only a freakin' fly,

and Titus is moving fast, pulling his sweatshirt on and tackling Adrian. "You threw it up there!" he cries, laughing. "So you go get it."

"Not me." Adrian giggles. "I didn't throw anything." They are laughing and play-fighting. "Did you see me throw anything, Malachy?" Malachy shakes his head and doesn't get involved.

"Ip, you liar, I saw you throw it—"

"No, it flew—"

"If you don't fetch it, I'm gonna make you eat it—"

"I'm just getting you back for third period—"

"Fetch it, you madman!"

"You fetch it, I have to be in class!" Adrian breaks free and runs, laughing and stumbling, into the gymnasium.

Titus sits on the floor for a minute, giggling helplessly as the rest of them troop in for hockey; then he drags the towel bin over to the locker, climbs up on the stack of dirty towels from earlier in the day and retrieves his shoe.

When class is almost over, I can hear Sanchez giving a pep talk from the other side of the gymnasium doors. He does that once in a while. Blows his whistle early, makes everyone sit on the floor, sweating, and gives a speech about "just doing it" or "being a team player" or "setting fitness goals."

It's crap.

This time, he's talking about junior year, and what our fitness goals should be over the summer, which is starting in eight weeks. Right now, he's saying, is the time to sign up for youth basketball league at a local community center, or start saving money to buy some weights, or arrange a weekly soccer game in the park. Keep fit all year round! Practice your skills!

Let's face it. No team from Ma-Ha is ever gonna win a championship. None of us artist-types is ever going to compete in the Olympics or play professional sports. Sanchez's goal isn't athletic excellence. He's just trying to make sure we have wholesome activities to distract us from the millions of degenerate things we could get up to in New York City.

As if playing soccer once a week is gonna stop you smoking crack if that's what you feel like doing.

Now Sanchez is lecturing on this requirement Ma-Ha has, starting junior year. Everyone has to try out for sports teams.

Everyone.

Even if they suck at sports. The only alternative is to take African dance, which a lot of girls do.

The gym program can't accommodate everyone for four years, so Ma-Ha makes us take it every day freshman and sophomore year, then forces all the juniors and seniors into after-school sports practice, and runs fewer gym classes for those grades, meaning upperclassmen only have to do gym two days a week instead of five.

"So think about your sports for next year!" cries Sanchez. "And come to me with any questions."

Everyone explodes into the locker room. It's such a din, I can only make out snips of what they're saying. Shane will do basketball and baseball; Adrian, baseball and swimming; Brat wants baseball too, but no one listens to him. Malachy thinks maybe fencing, likes basketball but knows he's probably too short. He talks to Shane about playing pickup games over the summer to improve his chances.

Titus dives in and out of the showers the way he did yesterday, and has on brown cords and a hooded black sweatshirt before I pay him any attention beyond a quick ogle of his narrow backside as he heads into the shower. Once he's dressed, he takes his time with his socks and boots, listening to Adrian talk about saving up for a baseball glove.

As they head out, he stays on the bench.

"You coming?" Adrian, near the door.

"Nah," says Titus. "I got stuff to do."

"You sure?"

"See you later."

"Whatever." Adrian and the others are gone.

Titus sits there on the bench for a couple of minutes. Just staring into space. Then he walks over to the mirror, the full-length one that the girls don't even have, and looks at himself.

He turns to the side and looks again. Runs his fingers through his hair. He pulls his sweatshirt up and looks at his pale white-boy stomach. His cords hang loose on his hips. He pulls the shirt up even farther, for a second, to see his hollow, hairless chest, then yanks it back down.

He's acting like a girl. Or like I thought only girls ever acted. Like he hates what he sees.

He grabs his pack and heads out the door.

Has Titus ever had a girlfriend?

I don't know.

I don't think so.

It was known across school that he liked Winifred last year, but I don't think they ever went out. And I've heard him and Adrian talk about girls like Cammie and Taffy; it seems obvious that he's interested. In girls, that is.

So why hasn't he been with anyone, then?

Malachy has gone out with lots of people. So has Adrian. Shane just got here this year, but he's been with me and now Jazmin. Even Brat, who's kind of a late-bloomer-type. He went out with a freshman girl last October for at least a couple of weeks.

But Titus—no one.

Wednesday. After an endless night spent waiting and hoping that come morning I'd find myself back in my human body, I wake from a half-sleep instead to find Brat, holding a cup of coffee and a muffin, sitting on a bench. The clock reads 7:34. He must be early to school.

He's just eating his breakfast and staring into space. When he's done with the muffin, he pulls a novel out of his backpack—*Ender's Game*—and reads while he finishes his coffee.

If they get to school early, most of the Art Rats hang out by the garbage cans, smoking cigarettes and talking. I've gone back there a couple times, first when I was seeing Shane and he was new and trying to get in with them—and then more recently when Katya started smoking and lurking around. But it's smelly, and I always feel shy and out of place, so I usually sit on the steps and draw in my sketchbook until the bell rings.

I always figured Brat was out back. But now I'm guessing he feels out of place too. Here in the locker room, I can see that the Rats barely talk to him, except for Malachy. They let him hang around, but they don't make any effort to include him. Like he's tolerated, but not fully one of them.

A couple minutes before the bell, Brat opens up his backpack and starts to rummage through it. I buzz down and sit next to him on the bench—he doesn't even notice me. His bag is just like his minilocker: jammed with stuff. Gym clothes and sketchbooks and books for class, of course, but also action figures and magazine clippings and tiny notebooks with drawings on the covers that probably contain more lists and notes like the ones I saw before.

He's like me. Like a boy version of me.
No wonder he doesn't fit in.

Brat finds what he's looking for—a comb—and pulls it through his scruffy red hair without even looking in the mirror. Then he slurps some water from the fountain and takes off.

The morning passes pretty much as usual. The juniors and seniors don't have class on Wednesdays, so the PE staff has a meeting first period. Sanchez and the basketball coach come in and talk shop while they pee. The second-period freshmen aren't much to look at.

After third period, Xavier and Carlo goof around and take showers. No Gunther today. Xavier is trying to get Carlo to talk to me—when I get back from wherever I am.

Could I ever go out with Carlo?

It wouldn't take much courage to start talking to him, if I ever get back in my human body. He's a sure thing.

And I could use a sure thing.

Yeah, he's an African-dance geek. But bring on the African dance geeks, as far as I'm concerned. It's ridiculous that in a school where everyone's trying to be such a unique individual,

I mean, people are wearing saris

and Pink Panther dolls

and smoking from forties cigarette holders for God's sake,

that guys still get crap for taking a freakin' dance class. Even me—I used to think they were wimps, prancing away with the girls instead of doing team sports—but now I can see they're only doing something they think is fun. Something I'd probably think is fun too.

Plus, they've got some guts, given the crap they've got to take just for doing contractions to a drumbeat.

What do I want in a guy, anyway?

I might be pretty happy dating a geek who can really shake it.

Late in the afternoon, Shane and Malachy are taking showers while the others are sitting on the benches, pulling on clothes.

"Yo!" Shane barks at Brat all of a sudden, switching off the water and wrapping a towel around his waist. "What are you looking at?"

"Huh?" says Brat. He might have been looking, but he might have just been thinking about something else, or tired from playing hockey.

"Don't be faggy," says Shane, turning off the water and grabbing his towel.

"I wasn't looking at you," says Brat.

"Oh yeah? Then what were you doing with your eyeballs, then?" interjects Adrian, boffing Brat on the back of the head with a dirty sweat sock. His tone is friendly, teasing. "Everyone saw you."

"I was—"

"You were looking, that's what."

"I know I'm gorgeous, booty boy," says Shane in a girly voice, pulling open his locker and getting out his clothes, "but this merchandise ain't for sale."

"Shut up," says Brat. "I was just thinking about something."

"Thinking about Shane's gherkin," says Adrian.

"Send it a letter," says Shane, laughing even though it doesn't make sense.

Adrian laughs too. "Dear Shane's gherkin," he says, also in a girly voice. "You're so fascinating, I can't take my eyes off you. Want to go for pizza after school? Yours sincerely, Bradley Parker."

"Dear Bradley Parker," answers Shane, in a deep masculine voice. "I belong to Jazmin LeMaitre, and believe me, she treats me good. I'm busy every day after school. And I do mean busy."

"Dear Shane's gherkin, Come on, one little date. I've been admiring you from afar!" Adrian laughs.

"Dear Bradley Parker," says Shane. "Leave me the fuck alone."

I cannot believe Shane is not only talking in the voice of his gherkin but having it discuss how good Jazmin treats it. Also acting like Brat is madly in love with it.

There's not even much to be in love with. By now, I should qualify as a gherkin expert, and his equipment isn't anything special. I mean, in a purely observational capacity, I've seen nearly a hundred gherkins every day for the past three days and I can attest that Shane's gherkin is a certifiably ordinary gherkin and he shouldn't be so cocky about it.

There is no big reason for Brat to be staring.

If you get what I mean.

It's funny. A week ago, it would have killed me to hear Shane

talking about messing around with Jazmin. Even yesterday, it
freaked me out when I saw them together in the hall, and I used
to hate having to sit in the same room with her during math and
art history. She was so slick, and so unaware of me, and yet I'd
sit there looking at her like she was my replacement,

because Shane thought she was better than me,

and so that meant she probably was better than me,

and I'd wonder—what's the secret of her sex appeal? Is it the
way she licks her lips, or the size of her biscuits?

And I'd think about them fooling around—

not because I wanted to, but because those stupid thoughts
would jump into my head—

and picture them hot on Shane's couch with the lights
all dim—

and I'd feel sick to my stomach and full of jealousy and ob-
session and rejection.

But now, when his gherkin is talking about how good Jazmin
treats it, and I know for sure he's going all the way with her or at
least doing oral, all I think is,

I'm glad it isn't me he's bragging about in the locker room.

Brat looks shocked when Shane says "Leave me the fuck
alone"—and it really is unfair for Shane to get mean about it,
since at this point it's Adrian who's putting all the focus on
Shane's gherkin, anyway.

Brat grabs his jacket from his locker and runs out of the
room. The sound of the swinging door echoes against the tiles.

"You didn't have to be such assholes just now." It's Malachy.

"What?" says Adrian. "We were kidding around."

"Brat's tough, he can take it," agrees Shane. "Besides, those eyeballs of his are always wandering."

"Who cares about his eyeballs?" says Malachy. "You don't have to pick on him."

"It was a joke," says Adrian. "He's gotta learn to take a joke."

"C'mon, Malachy. It was funny. Dear Shane's gherkin." Shane chuckles again as he pulls on his jeans.

"Brat didn't think so. I'm gonna catch him up. Later."

And Malachy is gone.

Shane and Titus and Adrian finish getting dressed.

Titus doesn't say anything at all. When he leaves, saying he's got homework and can't hang out after school, Adrian and Shane stand in front of the sinks for a minute, messing with their hair.

"He's freakin' out," says Adrian.

"Who, Titus?"

"Um-hm. About the sports thing next year."

"Well, he should freak. I love the guy, but he objectively sucks. It's like he's the most uncoordinated man on the planet."

"I know. Poor wuss."

"He's gonna end up like Gunther and those other geeks who have to take gym four days a week."

"You think?"

"That's what they do if you can't even qualify for JV bench. They make you take double gym."

"That sucks. Sanchez is such an ass."

"Titus should try swimming."

"Nah, he'll never make it. He barely floats."

"Did you see the poor guy cowering when Taffy came at him with the hockey stick?"

"She took that puck like taking candy from a baby."

Shane grins. "There's only one way out for him, then."

"What?" asks Adrian.

"African dance."

Wednesday night. In the deep darkness. From all the way across the room, I can hear the spider spinning new threads in her web.

The clock ticks.

A sink is leaking occasional drops of water onto the floor. One of the toilets runs funny.

There is no other sound.

The night is endless. I feel like I've been a fly forever.

I've got to turn back sometime. Somehow.

But how? And when? What if my fly body dies of old age before whatever powers made this happen reverse the spell?

Oh hell oh hell oh hell oh hell
Get me
out
of
here.

Someone.
Please.

thursday morning, I am grateful to be distracted by a new crop of seniors. Hugh is Monday/Tuesday gym. These guys are Thursday/Friday. I feel like it's Hanukkah—the new day brings new presents to unwrap.

Two guys come in early and steal a kiss inside a toilet stall, still wearing all their clothes. Then they head to different sides of the locker room and change for gym like nothing happened.

Like they're straight.

More filter in, and they change slowly, sluggishly. A couple of them wear their gym shorts to school and carry their jeans in their backpacks. Lots of them have coffee cups or soda cans, and when they go into class they leave them sitting on the sinks and benches, as if they'll only be gone for a minute.

I do like looking at them.
I do, I do.
Have I become a bad person, then?
I know I'd think badly of a guy for going to strip clubs or reading pervy magazines or spying on girls in the locker room. I'd think he was objectifying women or violating people's privacy.
But I'm doing it myself—the spying part—and I fully enjoy it.
And would it still be wrong if the guys knew about it and agreed to it—like if they were models or in a video?

Could I really be the type of girl who would buy a dirty video?

I don't know. I'm so full of hormones, anything seems possible.

I used to think beauty was something you could put your finger on. Of course, I knew it changed according to fashion—like long ago people used to prefer weak chins and rosebud mouths on women, whereas now we like strong jaws and wide grins; or good-looking men used to have big fuzzy sideburns that grew all the way down across their cheeks, and now that kind of facial hair looks mangy.

I know the svelte women we admire these days would have been considered scrawny things with no figures in previous centuries. But even so, I still thought: the good-looking people are the good-looking people. They are the ones people want to date, because good looks are what make people attractive. If a person has flaws, his rating goes down. Attractive is attractive is attractive.

And it turns out that's not so. Like what about Hugh? I think he's sexier now than I did when I'd only seen him with his clothes on—even though his clothes hide his bad skin and objectively there are problems with his body. He's sexy naked because he walks around in his argyle socks, drinking coffee. He's comfortable in himself.

Shane, on the other hand, looks great and has a gorgeous chest, but somehow seems hard and untouchable—like you're not really looking at him, but at a coat of armor he wears to keep people away. And Carlo looks better undressed than dressed, because his clothes are geeky. But his relatively nice body still doesn't do anything for me. He's got no milkshake—or whatever the equivalent is in boys.

Girls' magazines are always saying "confidence is the sexiest thing of all"—but even though that's kind of true for Hugh, Titus is the opposite. It's not his confidence that makes him sexy. He hasn't got any.

When he's got his clothes off, he seems even more naked than anyone else.

At the end of African dance, Xavier and Carlo don't come in right away. The drumbeats have stopped, but they're staying inside the gym for some reason.

Gunther arrives—first in his class as usual. He must have his third period in the sculpture studio right next door. He opens his minilocker and gets his sneakers, then sits down on a bench and starts to change.

I hear the voice of the drummer before I see him. He has a lilt—not African but Jamaican. He plays the bongos for the dance class, and he must arrive at the gym through the teachers' offices, because I've never seen him before. When he enters, Xavier and Carlo trailing behind him, I can see he's short, with shiny dark skin and dreads. Not dressed like a teacher—tan cords and a faded blue T-shirt. He's sweating a bit from playing the drums for so long.

"Is that the guy?" he asks Xavier.

Xavier nods. They must have told the teacher what's been going on with Gunther. And she sent the drummer in, to take care of stuff in the boys' locker room.

"Excuse me," says the drummer, standing over Gunther. "I wonder if I can talk to you for a second. My men here are having a problem and they asked me to step in and negotiate."

Gunther looks up. He's bigger than the drummer, but he's sitting down. "What do you want?" he asks.

"I'm hearing things about being pushed into lockers and threats and whatnot. Do you want to tell me what's been going on?"

"What did they say?"

"Look, no one wants any trouble. You want to give your side of the story?"

Gunther pulls on his sweatshirt. "I don't know what you're talking about. I'm minding my own crap."

"You haven't been intimidating my friends here? Because that's what I'm hearing. And that kind of thing can't be happening."

"I don't even know those guys. I got nothing to say."

"Oh," says the drummer, sounding innocent and sarcastic at the same time. "I'm very happy to hear that. Because I would hate to hear someone had been harassing my guys. If I heard any rumors like that again, I'd have to go talking to Mr. Sanchez about it, whereas right now we're keeping it between friends."

"You're barking up the wrong tree," says Gunther.

"I'm sure I am. A big man like you would never pick on someone who wasn't his own size. Let's chalk it up to nothing and say I'm happy to meet you." He smiles and extends his hand. "My name is David Mowatt. And you are?"

Gunther shakes, warily. "Gunther."

"Gunther what? So I can remember you next time I see you."

"Hocking-Delancy."

Mowatt lets go of his hand. "Nice to meet you, Gunther Hocking-Delancy. I hope we understand each other."

"Yeah, we understand each other," mutters Gunther.

"Good."

As if released from a spell, Xavier and Carlo scoot out from behind Mowatt and bang their lockers open. They grab their stuff, wave their thanks and run out into the hall.

Sophomore lunch, fifth period. The Thursday/Friday juniors and seniors who have gym now have already taken their hot, hairy bodies out for hockey, and the room is quiet. Usually, no one comes in while class is going on except an occasional guy on a hall pass who has to use the toilet, or the janitor to empty the towel bin; but today, I hear laughing from down the hall, and footsteps running, and Malachy comes barging through the door.

He stands still for a minute, looking around to make sure he's alone. Then he peeks under the bathroom stalls for people's feet, and quickly scouts behind the lockers for any lurking seniors. He pulls open the door to the hallway again and beckons someone in.

It's Katya.

Her hair is flowing down her back like she just brushed it, and she's wearing lip gloss. Malachy grabs her hand—they're both giggling—and starts kissing her.

Malachy is kissing Katya.

And it's clear they've done this before. Probably lots of times. His hands go right for her biscuits, and before long, her left hand is rubbing the front of his jeans.

Katya and Malachy.

Malachy and Katya.

I never even suspected, though I should have figured she had someone. She's been so evasive.

Duh: where has she been on weekend nights?

With Malachy.

Why can't I ever reach her on the phone?

She's with Malachy.

Why is she smoking cigarettes and eating lunch out back with the Art Rats, instead of with me?

To be with Malachy.

Why hasn't she had me over in ages, why is she always too busy?

She's been with Malachy.

But why didn't she tell me? I mean, we're best friends—aren't we?

After a few minutes, which I spend mainly buzzing around the ceiling trying not to watch this make-out session that is none of my business, Katya pushes Malachy away. "I'm thirsty," she says. "Just a second."

She heads over to the water fountain and drinks. He comes around and hugs her from behind. "Want to come to the end-of-April sculpture exhibit thing with me?"

"Hm." She stands up and walks over to the sinks, pulling her hair into a ponytail while she looks in the mirror. "It's probably not a good idea."

"Why not? People have gotta find out sometime."

"It's Gretchen," says Katya. "She'll be weird about it. She's so judgmental."

"You said that before. But who cares what Gretchen thinks?"

"I do."

"What, she doesn't like me?"

Katya hesitates. I think about all the times I've said Malachy was nothing much, that he never says anything and thinks having his ears pierced makes him slick. "No, she likes you all right," Katya lies. "But she doesn't know you. And she's all hung up about men. Like you guys are aliens or animals or something."

"We *are* animals," says Malachy, nuzzling her neck.

"I just feel like she'll be all mean about me having . . ." She pauses.

"A boyfriend," supplies Malachy. "I'm your boyfriend, right? So say it."

"Boyfriend," says Katya. "But she'll be mean about it, like I'm a traitor. And she'll say something dismissive."

"So?"

"So I'll know what she says is wrong, but I'll care what she thinks anyway—and then everything will have a taint on it."

"Katya, you worry too much. Just come with me now and walk down the hall and hold my hand."

Katya shakes her head.

"What's gonna happen?" Malachy asks. "Gretchen's not even in school."

"She'll hear about it anyway. She'll be mad I didn't tell her."

"So tell her, then."

"Not yet. I can't. She's still obsessed over what happened with Shane, and the two of you guys are friends, and . . . I just think she'll freak out. Trust me on this, okay?"

Malachy moves over to the window and stares at the frosted glass, right underneath where I'm perched. "You care more about what she thinks than you do about me."

"That's not it. Come on."

"I'm sick of sneaking around."

"Gretchen's been my best friend for two years. Don't ask me this."

"I am asking you," he says. "I am asking you this."

There's a rustle outside the door to the gymnasium. The juniors and seniors are heading back in to change their clothes. "I gotta go," says Katya, peeking out the door that goes to the hall, making sure no one will see her leave. "I'll call you later."

"Call me with an answer," Malachy shouts as she runs out.

Then he sits there,

like a statue,

while the older boys slap each other with towels and complain.

The Art Rats have finished showering after gym. Shane and Titus are talking about getting pizza. Malachy's eating a chocolate bar. Adrian is jumping on and off one of the benches for no apparent reason.

And I am thinking that the hierarchy they had at the start of the school year—with Titus at the top, then Malachy, then Adrian, Brat and Shane (the new guy)—has shifted now.

Today Shane, with his good looks and sports skills and hot girlfriend, is on top. And Brat's pushed to the bottom, even farther down than Shane ever was—because Shane doesn't like him. Then Malachy is one up from Brat.

Adrian, because he can keep up with Shane and since he's the "booty master," has got the number two slot. Which puts Titus in the middle at number three.

I wonder what he thinks of the shake-up.

Friday morning, at the end of third period, Gunther is waiting for Xavier and Carlo to come in after African dance. The bell hasn't rung yet; he must have cut out of sculpture early to be here. He's standing right by the gymnasium door, and as soon as Carlo enters, Gunther grabs him by the elbow and slams him against the wall. "You rat on me and you think that's gonna save you?" he grunts. "Some Mary Poppins teacher telling me to keep the peace?"

Xavier comes in, sweat glistening on his chocolate forehead, and sees Gunther all over Carlo. "Hey, what the—?"

Gunther's elbow is fast. He jabs it backward into Xavier's stomach, knocking him into the towel bin, which rolls across the floor. Xavier stumbles, but keeps his balance. "Why don't you leave us alone?"

Gunther doesn't say anything. He simply punches Carlo in the face, and as Carlo crumples to the floor in the corner by the door, he turns around to face Xavier. Blood is trickling from Carlo's mouth.

Xavier backs up, clearly frightened, and Gunther walks toward him menacingly. "You faggy little twerp," he says.

Xavier's right fist is clenched, like he's trying to get up the nerve to hit Gunther, but Gunther's not hesitating. He grabs Xavier's T-shirt in one hand, yanks him forward and hits his nose with an open palm. There's a crack, like Xavier's nose is breaking, and he collapses backward into a locker.

Carlo is on his feet again, and he runs at Gunther, trying to tackle him to the ground. But Gunther is stronger than both of them combined, and though he hits the floor when Carlo runs into him, it's only a second before he's sitting on Carlo's chest, delivering a solid punch to the neck. Carlo's head lolls to the side, and Xavier jumps on Gunther, trying to pull him off.

But Gunther is a smart fighter. He's done with Carlo, and he lets Xavier pull him up, only to flip around and slam him up against the full-length mirror, cracking it from top to bottom. Small pieces of glass splinter onto the tiles. "You shut the fuck up about me," says Gunther, his face close to Xavier's. "You keep your faggy ass out of my business, like I told you. You understand?"

Xavier nods in fear, his eyes looking over at Carlo, who's not moving.

Then Gunther knees Xavier in the balls and tosses him to the floor like a used tissue. As both boys lie there, moaning, he grabs his pack and bangs out into the hallway.

Everything is silent for a minute. Then Carlo sits up on his elbows, moving his neck gingerly, as if he feels like his head might fall off his body. "Fuck."

"Yeah, fuck," moans Xavier.

"So much for your stupid David Mowatt plan," says Carlo.

"Yeah, so much for it."

"Fuck, he split my lip."

"I think he broke my goddamn nose, motherfucker."

Carlo sits up and scootches on his butt over to where Xavier is lying. "Nah. It's bloodied up, but you're not gonna have a badass boxer nose or anything."

Xavier sits up. "Your lip is swelling like you got Botox."

"Collagen."

"What?"

"It's collagen that they put in their lips."

"Whatever."

They chuckle and sit there in silence.

I wonder if they've been beaten up before.

Then Xavier says, "We better get out before anyone comes in and asks us about the glass. What you got now, math?"

"Yeah."

"You wanna skip it and get lunch?"

"Yeah," says Carlo. "I want that sushi from the little takeout place."

"I want papaya drink," says Xavier. "And a monster hot dog." He gets to his feet slowly and offers his hand to Carlo, who takes it and stands up carefully, as if his head hurts. "Let's go."

And with a quick glance in the broken mirror at their own mangled faces, they are gone.

Seconds later, the bell rings and the rest of the juniors start coming in for class. Gunther comes back, moving stiffly, and kids around with his friends as he puts on his clothes.

I'm so mad, I don't know what to do.

There's nothing to do.

Would be nothing even if I had my human body.

I could tell a teacher, sure, but there's no explanation for how I know what I know—and even if someone believed me and Gunther got suspended, he'd just come back and beat the crap out of Xavier and Carlo again later.

It's stuff like this that makes me love comic books so much. Because in real life, we are powerless. Guys like David Mowatt can step in and try to help, but in the end, they don't do any good. In the Marvel Universe, though, a person can make a difference.

A person can save the world.

eighth period, the Art Rats come in. Shane and Adrian are throwing a basketball back and forth over the top of the set of lockers. Malachy is sulking a bit; he shoves a chocolate kiss into his mouth as he changes clothes, then heads into the gym while the others goof around.

Titus and Brat are a little late, eating red licorice. They probably ran off campus in between the bells to buy it.

"Hey, fags, where you been?" says Adrian, tossing the ball to Titus.

"Give some over," pleads Shane, in that way he has that lets him say something extremely bossy while still sounding sweet.

"Oh, yeah, me too," says Adrian, hopping toward Titus with only one shoe on.

Titus gives them each a rubbery red stick. "Buy your own, you bottom-feeders," he laughs.

"I'm no bottom-feeder," says Shane, making a mock muscle that still shows off his real ones. "I'm all man."

"Yeah, me neither," adds Adrian, chewing.

"You half-wit," says Titus. "A bottom-feeder is a fish. Like a fish that lives off particles that other fish drop."

Adrian laughs. "Not in my book."

"A bottom-feeder," says Shane, "is a species of animal most often found in Chelsea wearing leather and a dog collar. It's called a bottom-feeder because . . ." He pauses.

"What?" asks Brat.

"It's too disgusting to describe if you don't know what it is already." Shane shakes his head.

138

"What?"

"No, it's too faggy," says Shane. "I'll lose my lunch."

I'm sure he's making this up on the spot. There's no gay-sex-thing bottom-feeder. But just like with the gherkin letter, Adrian falls right in with Shane's joke: "Trust me, you innocents. You don't want to know."

"I know the bottom is a subject of great interest to you, personally," Shane says, affecting a kind and explanatory manner and putting his hand on Brat's shoulder like a teacher.

"Fuck off, it is *not*," says Brat, shoving Shane away and starting to get into his gym clothes.

"But the feeding part," Shane continues, his face cracking into a smile, "is a metaphor! Or a simile, or whatever." He collapses in giggles. "Go down to Chelsea and figure it out."

"I just asked a question," says Brat. "Crap."

"Oh, sorry, you're a gherkin man," laughs Shane. "I should have remembered. Then we'll have to hook you up with some bottom-feeders, if you know what I mean." More laughter. "Oops, you *don't* know what I mean!"

The bell rings. They're late.

All of them throw on their gym clothes hastily. Brat is looking down at the floor, his mouth tight like he's trying not to cry, and Shane lopes over and elbows him gently in the side. "Just messing with you, little guy. Don't take it hard," he says, and Brat smiles weakly.

Titus grabs his shoes from his minilocker and runs into the gym carrying them, sliding the last yard before the door in his sock feet, taking advantage of the slick tile.

Titus
Titus
Titus
I love that you skid in your socks.

And for forty-five minutes, hockey pucks slam against the rubberized gym walls.

After class, Titus is the first guy in. He's out of his shorts and in the shower before the next person gets there, and in seconds he's shaking the water out of his hair, turning off the faucet and wrapping a towel around himself.

As always, he's like a raw nerve without his clothes on. Like he's only comfortable in his head, not his body. Like the bright fluorescent light of the locker room physically hurts him—the way it invites scrutiny, the way it glints off the other guys' broad shoulders and muscular legs.

Once he gets his jeans and shirt on, he's usually back to normal—but this time, he still looks nervous. He sits on a bench by the lockers, staring into space and ignoring the chaos around him. Like he's gearing up for something.

And he is.

When Shane and Adrian are nearly dressed, Titus says to Adrian in a low voice, "That was so uncool, what you and Shane were doing."

"What?"

"Earlier, that whole bottom-feeder crap."

"Me?" says Adrian. "I hardly said anything."

"Not to Brat, maybe, but you're always saying that shit."

"Like what?"

"Gay shit."

"Get off. That's between Shane and Brat. He just gives him a hard time 'cause he's such a junior fag about everything. Talk to Shane if you're pissed, but believe me, Brat's okay. He can take it."

"I don't want to talk to Shane," says Titus, although Shane is right there and can hear every word. "I'm talking to you."

Brat is sitting still now, on the other side of the bank of lockers, just out of view. Listening. They obviously think he's gone.

"All right then," sighs Adrian. "Spill."

Titus is silent for a moment. Then he says, "What did you mean just now, 'junior fag'?"

Adrian looks surprised. "Nothing."

"Are you saying Brat's gay?"

"I'm not saying anything about who he likes, or whatever. He's just a wimp: he never stands up for himself."

"Okay, then. That's my point," says Titus.

"What?"

"Brat's—whatever. I'm not talking about Brat, really, at all."

"Then what the hell are you talking about?" asks Adrian. Malachy is listening now too.

"You're always saying this homophobic crap," Titus bursts out. "Like 'Meadows is a faggot' for giving us homework, or 'Titus was so gay in hockey,' or 'Don't be faggy, loan me a dollar.' Hell, Ip, you wouldn't take it for a second if someone called you a Chink, and I know you beat up that guy who said 'bucket head'—

so why are you talking about gay people like being queer is the worst shit anyone could ever be?"

"I'm not talking about gay people," says Adrian defensively. "It's a way of talking. It's just how I talk, okay? It doesn't mean anything."

"But it does."

"What, Titus, are you gay?" Shane breaks in.

"No, I'm not fucking gay. But you don't know who is, or who isn't, and you're saying 'fag this' and 'fag that'—all the time, where anyone can hear you."

"Oh, come on," says Shane. "You can tell when someone is gay."

"No. You can't," barks Titus. And then, lower-key: "Ip, you're my friend, right?"

"Yeah." Adrian looks surprised to hear this, in the middle of being yelled at.

"Why do you think I don't have you at my house, huh? Why, when I live five blocks from school and you're always trying to invite yourself over?"

"Crap, I don't know," says Adrian.

"Because my dad's boyfriend is there when I get off school, that's why," says Titus. "Matt. Matt Levine. He teaches at NYU, so he's home a lot. And you tools would make stupid-ass gay jokes, and talk about your gherkins and how Matt shouldn't look at them—like he'd even want to—and then my dad would get home and they'd hug or something and you'd say some crap about it that would be so stupid and offensive I wouldn't be able to be friends with you anymore." Titus stops and draws a shaky

142

breath. "So I fucking *don't* have you over, and I leave the whole thing in the closet, and everything's fine except you have to run your stinking mouth off about faggots all the time until I can't fucking stand it anymore. Because I live in the faggot house. All right? All my dad's friends are gay, except for a couple people he knows from the hospital. We've got gay books, and gay pictures on our fridge, and it's all too freakin' *gay* for you, Adrian, and I don't want you over at my house talking your crap about my family."

"Hey, Titus," says Shane. "Chill out. Nobody meant anything."

"Don't get me started on *you*," barks Titus, turning on Shane. "You're way the hell worse than he is"—gesturing at Adrian.

Shane holds his hands up as if in surrender. "Whoa. I was just kidding around."

"Don't get so mad," says Adrian. "No one meant anything."

Malachy is silent. Brat is still hidden behind the lockers on the other side, unmoving.

Titus doesn't say anything. He grabs his jacket out of his locker and stuffs it in his backpack. Just to have something to do with his hands.

Adrian tries again. "Titus. Hey. I really never thought about it that way."

Titus is silent.

"I'm sorry, all right? I get what you're saying."

No response.

"Come on, answer me. You're making me feel like crap."

Nothing.

"Shane's gherkin is sorry, too," says Adrian. "It wants to send you a letter of apology."

Nothing again.

"You know how it likes to write letters. It's writing a whole freakin' opus already, it's so sorry."

Still silence.

"Even *my* gherkin is sorry, and it didn't talk shit about anybody," persists Adrian.

The edge of Titus's mouth quivers in laughter.

"Listen to this: how 'bout I promise to watch my goddamn motherfucking big-ass mouth?" says Adrian. "From here on out."

Titus cracks a smile.

"I won't say any shit that's fucking offensive. You can drag me around by my balls if I do." Adrian's giggling a bit now, but I can tell he means it.

"All right," says Titus. "What the fuck."

"I'll be a fucking politically correct choirboy, you'll see." Adrian reaches over and socks him on the arm. "Then maybe you'll have me over to watch the TiVo."

"Yeah, maybe." Titus laughs. "You still gonna vacuum?"

And it seems like things are okay.

Adrian looks at his watch. "I have to work at four. I'm gonna scoot. We all right?"

Titus sighs. "We're all right."

Adrian jerks his head at Shane. "You taking the train?"

Shane nods and throws his pack over his shoulder. "Catch

you later," he says to Titus—and it's hard to tell if he's mad, or sorry, or what.

Malachy follows them out, and Titus slumps down on the bench with his elbows on his knees. After a minute, Brat starts bustling around in the back of the room, running some water and pulling his wet hands through his hair.

"Hey," says Titus, like he knew Brat was there all along.

"Hey yourself."

"What a drama."

"Ain't life without it," says Brat, flicking the water off his hands and walking toward Titus.

"Guess not."

Brat sits down. They are quiet for a minute. "You know I like boys."

"I kinda figured," says Titus.

"Even when I went out with Sallie?"

"Yeah."

Brat picks at his fingernails. "You're the first person I told."

Titus sighs. "Well, Shane probably has a clue."

"God, all he thinks about is his gherkin," complains Brat. "I mean, I'm queer and I don't think about gherkins nearly as much as him."

"Nobody could," laughs Titus. "He's obsessed. He's like a gherkin maniac, that guy."

"Queer. I never said that before," says Brat.

"We're here, we're queer, get used to it."

"What?"

"It's a thing they chant at marches," explains Titus. "Or at the gay pride parade, or whatever."

"You go to gay pride parades?"

"It's like the family religion. I get unbelievable crap from my dad if I don't go."

Brat stands again. "We're here, we're queer, get used to it. Well, that was excellent, what you said before."

Titus looks away like he doesn't want to deal. "It's done."

the after-school sports guys filter in and out again. I am trying to resign myself to the weekend as a fly with nothing to do and no one to even watch, much less talk to, when Malachy bangs through the door. He throws his pack on the ground and goes quickly into one of the toilet stalls.

Normally I don't look at the boys in there. I mean, there's nothing to see anyhow (no one has flogged the gherkin at school or anything like that), and I figure that even the worst voyeur, which I fully admit that I am, can grant them their privacy in the stalls. But Malachy isn't on the john. He's standing in there crying. I hear the snuffling, and buzz over to see him clutching a wad of toilet paper with his hands over his face.

I've never seen a guy cry. Not even my dad.

Eventually, he comes out and splashes some water on his face. Then he pulls a notepad out of his pack and starts to write.

"About today, you need to stop making other people your priority and—"

He rips the page out of the book and crumples it up next to him.

"Katya, think about it again—"

This one he crosses out with a dark slash, and turns the page.

"I've thought about it and however you want things to be is how they'll be. Will you—"

He crosses this one out too, and sits looking at a fresh page, fiddling with his pen.

God, I want my body back. Want to stop being this someone else, this fly, and be Gretchen Yee again.

Not just for the obvious reasons, like

I want to kiss Titus and

eat tofu with black bean sauce and

I remember how good it feels to have a soft charcoal drawing pencil in my hand and

I want to take hot showers in the morning and

read a big stack of new comic books and

listen to my dad laugh and

breathe the smells of New York City as I walk down the street, but also because I could fix this for Malachy. If Katya's broken up with him because of what she thinks I'll say, I can tell her that I know about the two of them. I can be happy for her.

She was right, I think, about what I would have done if I had found out earlier. I would have been mad and freaked out about all the boys who don't like me back,

and what might happen to our friendship.

I would have felt like she'd betrayed me,

already did feel like it, actually, from her not being there all the time and hiding something from me—

but I don't feel that way anymore.

Katya's got a boyfriend. A nice one, who hangs with Brat when everyone else is ignoring him, who writes her notes, who cries over her and wants to take her out to places and hold her hand in public.

She's lucky.

She shouldn't lose him over me.

I will never save the world. And I will never be a superhero. But I could do something to make at least two people happier than they are right now, if only I were Gretchen Yee, back in my life where I belong.

part three

life as a superhero

after a night of no dreams at all, I wake up in my bed.

My bed.

My bed! A big double bed containing several comic books, a copy of "The Metamorphosis," a dirty T-shirt, way too many baby dolls, some cookie crumbs and me. A human girl wearing pajama bottoms and a cotton camisole.

I stretch my arms, wonderful arms, to the ceiling and look at them.

They have hands.

They have opposable thumbs.

I rub them on my face, feeling my skin, my eyes, my lips. They're all there, familiar and new at the same time.

Suddenly, I'm up and in front of the mirror. I'm looking at myself and jumping up and down, holding my biscuits to keep them from bouncing, and squealing like I'm seeing a long-lost friend.

Me
me
me
me

I flip on the radio and dance around like a maniac, waving my arms and shaking my butt and feeling the glorious rug under my toes. Then I put on some sweats and running shoes, grab my keys and two twenties off the kitchen table and run out the door.

It's early, and the air is still morning-chilly, but the sky is bright. I run down the empty sidewalk, past shuttered drugstores and bodegas, past all-night diners with the stale-coffee smell wafting out, past little shops that sell cheap plastic toys and religious icons. I plan on running over to the East River, breathing the air and looking through my only-two eyes and stretching my only-two legs—but I've only gone four blocks when I pass a bakery that's open. A little chic French place that only in New York City would be squashed in between a decrepit check-cashing place and the Off-Track Betting. They're brewing espresso in there, I can smell it, and buttery croissants are lined up in the window.

All I've eaten this week is some bits of stray muffin people dropped on the floor, part of a potato chip and some spilled ginger ale. Flies barf on their food to soften it up and then suck it in through their tube-mouths, so eating anything at all was gross as hell, and I only did what I absolutely had to to keep alive.

I finger the twenties in my pocket and go into the bakery. Two almond croissants, a fresh-squeezed orange juice and a hot chocolate later, I am convinced that the existence of French pastry and Florida fruit is enough to make anyone happy to be alive.

I head to the drugstore and buy three boxes of tissues, two bottles of cough medicine, some more orange juice and some Cold Comfort tea. At home, I tip the contents of one of the medicine bottles into the toilet and leave the sticky, empty container on the bathroom sink. I put the other one on the table by my bed. I fill a couple of glasses partway with OJ and leave them around the apartment. Half the tea goes in the incinerator, and the open box goes on the kitchen counter. I crumple most of the tissues into little balls and fill all our garbage cans with them.

I listen to the answering machine.

Ma, sounding happy, calling from Marianne's cell phone. She's sorry again that she yelled at me before she left, she loves me, she's wearing sunblock so don't worry, and don't try to call her back because there's pretty much no reception anyway.

Katya, checking to see if I'm sick, since I'm not in school.

My Chinese grandmother, who lives in D.C., hanging up on the answering machine, but I know it's her.

Pop from Hong Kong, reminding me he'll be home by noon on Saturday.

I delete everything and look in the fridge. There's some leftover takeout, and I smear it on a stack of plates and put them into the sink. I consider crumpling up clean clothes and putting them in the laundry hamper, but my dad isn't *that* observant.

It's still early, but I call Katya anyway. Mrs. Belov picks up and I can hear the little monsters laughing in the background, plus the sound of the television and Mr. Belov saying something in Russian. It takes Katya a minute to come to the phone. I must have woken her up.

"Where have you been?" she mumbles.

"I had the worst cold. My snot was green."

"Ugh. Way too much information."

"Sorry," I say. "I went through two of those giant things of NyQuil. Anyway, I didn't call you back because I had no voice until yesterday. I had to buy that throat spray where you spray it in and it makes you numb. It was the darkest day. I was so sick I couldn't get dressed. I went to the drugstore in my pajamas."

Katya laughs. "Did you wear shoes, or go in slippers?"

"Slippers. It was pitiful. My parents aren't even back yet so I was all alone. I didn't shower for four days."

"Poor Gretch."

"Well," I say, cheerfully. "I feel human again now. What happened at school?"

Katya lets out a squeal. "You won't believe it. Taffy brought in a topless self-portrait. We had to do full-body, looking in a mirror, and she did topless."

I laugh. That is so Taffy. "Did you see the biscuits and everything? Or was it like atmospheric in shadow?"

"You couldn't see nipple. She had her arms crossed over her chest, like she's so modest. All you could really see was like the edge of one biscuit."

"She's not that well endowed."

"Hey, a biscuit is a biscuit," says Katya. "You are so sorry you missed Adrian's face. His tongue was on the floor. I swear he almost fell down."

"Why would she go topless?"

"Oh, she got exactly what she wanted."

"What?"

"Adrian's tongue hanging out."

"Can you imagine if Cammie did that?" I ask. "It would be a state of emergency. Because there's no way her arms can hide those biscuits. Every single guy in the whole class would be catatonic."

"Biscuit-induced comatosis," says Katya. "And the floor would be covered in drool. They'd have to call the janitors in to wipe it up so no one would slip."

"And special forces would have to come in to roll all the tongues back into the boys' mouths."

She laughs.

"Hey, what are you doing tonight?" I ask. "Do you want to get cake at that place in Soho?"

"I can't," says Katya. "I think I have to babysit."

"You think, or you know?"

"I'm pretty sure I do."

"Ask your mom, then—isn't she right there?"

"She's making breakfast for the monsters, I don't want to interrupt her."

"Katya."

"I'll ask her later."

"Katya!"

"What?"

"You're not babysitting," I say.

"What? I swear, I am."

"You're going out with Malachy."

She is silent for a second. "No. Malachy and me are through. I'm too depressed to go out."

"Oh."

"How did you know?"

"Last Friday," I say, "from the way you talked about him. And the way he looked at you in the hall. And the way you're always busy now."

"Yeah." Katya's voice is heavy. "Sorry I didn't tell you. I didn't think you'd approve."

"Why not?"

"I don't know. Anyway, it doesn't matter now. We had this big fight and I broke up with him."

"How come?"

"Oh, it's so involved. Let me switch phones." The line crackles, and I listen to the monsters yelling in Russian until Katya picks up the phone in her parents' bedroom and yells, "Hang it up in there!" and finally, someone does.

"Yeah, well," she says, as if she's changed her mind. "I don't think I can explain it. We've been going out together a long time, actually."

"Since when?"

"Since winter break," she says. "Remember you

couldn't come to the big Hanukkah thing my family had? Well, I ran into him the day before, and I kind of mentioned the party, and he showed up with a box of almond cookies. That's how it started. No one else from school was there."

"He's a great guy, Katya. I really think so."

"You do?"

"Yeah. I mean, he's quiet and I don't really know him, but haven't you seen how he's nice to Brat when all the Rats blow him off? And he's an amazing artist. Not a show-off like Shane and Adrian, he doesn't strut around like he's all that. He's just himself, if that makes sense." Now I feel awkward. "There aren't a lot of guys like that."

"Ugh." Katya laughs bitterly. "Don't tell me that now. I'm being mad at him."

"Sorry. Do you want to say why?"

She thinks. "No. I guess not. I'm sorry I didn't tell you about it before."

"That's okay," I say.

"You know what?" she says, suddenly sounding brighter. "Now I'm changing my mind. Maybe I'll call him."

"You should."

"Okay, I'm going to."

"Right now?"

"Yeah. Before I lose my nerve. I'll call you back."

And she hangs up.

Half an hour later, she rings to say everything's better. They're together again.

When my dad's key turns in the lock at twelve-thirty, I'm back in bed, back in my pajamas, reading comic books and drinking juice.

I'm still mad at him but I'm glad to see him anyway. He stands in the doorway of my room, wearing a trench coat and holding his computer bag.

"Oh, Gretch," he says first thing. "Are you sick?"

"I was out all week. I didn't want to get you worried, so I didn't call." I give the green-snot, can't-speak, drugstore-in-my-pj's story. It goes over big.

"I brought you something." He comes and sits on my bed.

"What?"

"From the toy convention."

He pulls a bag of small, clear plastic boxes out of the outside pocket of his bag. Inside each one is a Bean Curd Baby. "It's the new generation," he says. "You can't get them over here yet."

They are perfect. I love them. Even though I haven't collected them since I was fourteen.

Ma would never buy me these. She always wants me to be interested in literature and rare books and the history of the Puritans. Pop sucks in lots of ways—but he knows what I like and he doesn't think it's stupid.

I lean in to kiss him on the cheek,

and he smells like cigarettes again.
Why would he smell like them now?
He just got off the plane.
He can't have gone to Hong Kong with the other woman, can he?
But he must have—
He must have just left her—
Hell, they've shared a smoke-filled cab from the airport.
Couldn't he stay away from his chippie at least until Ma and I got out of the freakin' house?
Does he have to make a sex holiday out of a legitimate business trip when his wife is still picking up his dry cleaning?
Hell—

and then an open pack of Camels falls out of his coat pocket. It's lying on my rug. He's talking about how the new generation Bean Curd Babies also include Bean Curd Pets, and he tries to bend down and get them as if nothing happened, but I'm too fast for him and I pick them up.

"What, Pop, why do you have these?"

He looks stunned. "Uh, yeah, Gretch, I—"

"What?"

"I started again when Ma and I began talking about the divorce."

"They're yours?"

"Yes."

"You're not holding them for a friend?"

"No. You know, I smoked in college—"

"What?"

"Oh yeah," he says. "Three packs a day, actually. Nicotine fiend. I gave it up right before you were born, and I didn't touch them again for seventeen years. But I've been so unhappy about everything here. I mean, I haven't talked about it with you, I didn't want you getting upset, and anyway, Ma and I had an argument one day and I went out to get some air, and before I knew it I had bought a pack. Now I'm up to a pack and a half a day," he sighs. "I didn't want you to know. It's such a bad example."

"You should quit, Pop," I say.

"I know, but I can't do it right now. I don't think you know how sad I am these days, Gretch."

He's not having an affair.

Late nights and a lost tie: there have always been late nights. He runs his own company. And he's definitely one for losing things. Keys, wallets, receipts, pens. They go missing every day.

There is no someone else. No chain-smoking chippie on the side.

My dad is not a cheater.

He's a smoker.

Just a regular person who can't get along with his wife anymore and takes up an old bad habit.

"I kind of know," I say. How sad he is.

He kisses me on top of my head and heads down the hall to take a shower. When he's done, we walk across town to see his new apartment. He smokes three cigarettes on the way, looking into space as he lights each one, like he's trying to pretend he's not doing it in front of me.

The place is tiny—one room and a galley kitchen, but it has a long, exposed brick wall that runs from one end to the other. "I want to build shelves here," Pop says, waving his arms. "Floor to ceiling."

"Ooh!" I nearly yell.

"What?"

"You know how Ma is on me to get rid of all my stuff, my comics and all that?"

"I couldn't miss it."

"Well, what if I stored some of it here? When you build the shelves? I mean, I know there's not a bedroom, but couldn't I keep some stuff here?"

He says yes, and we go right away to this big store down the block where they sell containers and boxes for almost anything you could ever think of. He buys me ten plastic bins and a set of magazine boxes for the comic books, and we arrange to have them delivered to the old apartment. Then we pick up Chinese at this amazing place on Twenty-fourth and Ninth, and walk home fast.

When the food is eaten, we go in my room together and sort through some of my stuff. Pop's excited about the plates of plastic Chinese food; he wants to display them on his shelves, so we put them in a cardboard box to go to his apartment. Then the doorbell rings with the container delivery, and we put the collectible comics, the action figurine collection, the Pez dispensers, the *Fangoria* backlog, the jars of plastic characters (Anti-Potato, Bean Curd Babies, etc.) and the Hong Kong travel souvenirs all into stacking bins and magazine boxes so they can go live at his place.

Pop helps me pick up the spilled paper clips and the tissue packets, then convinces me to throw out the box of glitter eye shadow.

We shove the stuffed animals and the baby dolls into the laundry machines in the basement. They fill three washers. When they're clean, I keep Yellow Baby and Rollo, plus my old teddy bear, and put the rest in a bag for the Salvation Army store. I know it's stupid, but I whisper goodbye to them and tell them I love them.

When we declare ourselves done, my floor is still covered with art supplies, shoes and clothes. My shelves still have all my old picture books on them, plus the chapter books, six stacks of noncollectible comic books and a whole lot of stuff not even worth mentioning.

But I feel lighter.

Pop goes to bed early because he's jet-lagged. I do the full-length portrait assignment Katya told me about, so I won't be massively behind in Kensington's class.

Head,
ear,
shoulders,
shirt.
I am not sharing my biscuits with the whole art class, thank you very much.
Legs,
fabric of jeans,
and feet.
It is reasonably like me. A figure of a girl with her chin tilted up. I look like I'm gazing into the sky.
With shading and detail, it's semilikely to please Kensington, since there are no panels, no hard edges and no hyper-muscled superheroes.
But:
I don't really want to please Kensington
after all,
now
do I?

So I add a huge, ornate pair of wings to my self-portrait. I shade the figure, and add the details of my shirt pocket and my bracelets, and the clip in my hair. But I concentrate most of my effort on the wings, making them transparent and fragile, but also strong and aerodynamic.

I am a winged girl.

I spend Sunday afternoon down in Brighton Beach with Katya. We walk along the boardwalk and she tells me how she snuck into Malachy's apartment last night after everyone was asleep, and they made out on his bed for nearly two hours.

She's got a hickey on her neck.

I tell her about the divorce.

Ma won't be home until Tuesday, but I buy her some Russian candy as a coming-home present. They have it in big bins upstairs in one of the grocery stores, wrapped in brightly colored paper and marked with writing I don't understand.

At home, Pop cooks dinner, and we avoid discussing Ma, or the move, or anything heavy. I spend some time on the computer while he does the dishes, and then we watch TV until I'm falling asleep on the couch.

Monday morning, I wear the red vinyl miniskirt that's been lying on the floor of my closet ever since I bought it.

Milkshake.

I'm at school early, and I don't go sit on the steps with my coffee and my sketchbook, the way I usually do. I walk around the block to the back of the building where the garbage cans are.

No one's there yet except Brat. He's got coffee and a muffin and *Ender's Game* and a cigarette and he's multitasking unsuccessfully. He ends up with some ash on his muffin.

"Hey, Brat."

"Gretchen. You been out sick?" His face is toward the sun, so he squints.

I go through my green-snot drugstore-in-pajamas story.

"You missed some high drama," he says.

"Katya told me about Taffy and her biscuits."

"Yeah. She took crap about it, but it's like it rolls right off her. I guess she likes the attention." He looks down at his coffee and swirls it around. "Hey, here's one you don't know. Shane and Titus got in a fistfight Saturday. We were all down in Battery Park. Them and me and Ip and Malachy."

"A fight like they were punching each other?"

"Well, Titus only put his hands up to his chest to

defend himself, but Shane really swung. Titus has a black eye." He exhales a cloud of smoke. "Your friend Titus fights like—"

"Don't say 'like a girl.' "

"Like a mouse," laughs Brat. "He got his ass kicked."

"What was it about?"

"I don't know. Some macho crap."

I'm sure he's lying, but that's okay. "Are they friends again?"

Brat shrugs. "I'm guessing not. We had to get ice from a guy with a hot dog cart to put on Titus's eye. Shane took off."

"Hell," I say. "One week and everything changes."

We are quiet for a minute. I can see Malachy down at the corner, heading our way. "Wanna see something my dad brought me from Hong Kong?" I ask.

Brat nods.

I pull out two Bean Curd Babies from my bag. "You know what these are?"

"Oh, wow. Is that the new generation?" says Brat, his voice excited. "I read on the Web they have pets, too. Did he bring you the pets?"

And we talk Bean Curd Babies as people arrive and light up around us—until I remember that I have to see the principal before class.

I head into Valenti's office with a note from my dad. It says I had a nasty bout of the flu, my parents were out of town, he's so sorry he didn't notify the school about it earlier, and of course I am planning to make up all the work.

"Hm," says Valenti when I hand her the note. "I trust you're feeling better now, Miss Yee?"

"Yes."

"I've got your transcript here," the principal says, pulling a file from her drawer. "Your academic record isn't in great shape."

"I know," I say. "I have to get myself together."

"Attendance at the Manhattan High School for the Arts is a privilege," Valenti continues, "and I want to see my students striving to reach the high bar we set. This spotty record doesn't speak well for your commitment to the visual arts or to your academic studies. . . ."

She goes on, a speech I'm sure she delivers a hundred times a year to degenerate students of various kinds.

"Um, excuse me?" I venture, when the lecture seems to be winding down. "There *is* something I want to talk to you about. Since I'm here."

"Yes? I'm listening." Valenti puts on a sympathetic face, like she's all set to listen to a story about me doing drugs or being pregnant.

I take a deep breath. "Can you tell me the ratio of students at this school? Like how many girls there are, compared to how many boys?"

"Certainly," she answers, looking a bit surprised.

"The student body is fifty-two percent female, forty-eight percent male."

"It is?" I say. "Because it has, ah, come to my attention—I mean, not that I've ever been in there, but I was talking to some people, and it seems like the girls' locker room is only like half the size of the boys'. They've got twice as many showerheads as we do, more bins for dirty towels, more toilet stalls and urinals on top of that."

"Go on."

"Well, I hear they've got a full-length mirror in there, and some minilockers to keep their shoes in overnight, or shampoo, or whatever, and also full-height lockers so they can hang their coats up."

Valenti leans back in her chair and crosses her arms. "I see."

"I was talking to my dad about it," I go on, "and he said Title Nine makes it illegal to have sex discrimination in sports programs at a school that gets government funding. Which we must be getting, right? Because this is a public school."

"Title Nine," says Valenti.

I look down at the Post-it note in my hand. "Yeah. Title Nine of the Education Amendments of 1972."

"I know what Title Nine is, Miss Yee."

"Oh." Because she really had sounded like she didn't. "So, it's more than thirty years since it became illegal to give girls only half the space that boys get in the locker rooms, plus worse facilities like smaller lockers and no minilockers."

She's silent.

"I'm right, aren't I? Because equal treatment means supplies and practice times and scholarships, but also locker rooms. I looked it up on the Web. And, um, like I said, it's been more than thirty years and we still have these tiny-ass locker rooms and it's just wrong. I'd like to make a complaint."

Hell. I can't believe I said "tiny-ass" right in front of the principal.

Is she gonna throw me out for disrespect?

Valenti sighs heavily and leans forward. "You know, Miss Yee, it's a good point. This building was built in the 1950s, before Title Nine existed, when it was commonplace to have unequal facilities. Girls participated very little in athletics and team sports back then. In my day"—and here, Valenti actually cracks a smile—"the only sports girls did were volleyball and cheerleading."

"But now," I blurt out, "you're *making* us do gym five days a week and we have to play a sport starting junior year. And it is just too stupid crowded in there."

"I'd like to be in compliance with Title Nine," says Valenti, "but where is the money going to come from?

Even should we apply for additional government money or raise funds from the PTA to remodel, we'd have to cut into the sculpture studio in order to make space for the expanded locker room—and the studio is too small as it is. Believe me, Miss Yee, I'm aware of the inequality; I just don't see what there is to do about it. Take space from the arts program that is the premise of our school, or leave things as they are. And that's not even considering where the money is to come from, and whether a big remodeling project is the best possible allocation of funds, considering the fact that we're undersupplied with basics like textbooks."

"Oh."

"Yes," says Valenti. "Now you can see why things stand as they do. Thank you for bringing it to my attention, but unless something major happens in terms of funding, I'm afraid it's impossible."

"It's so unfair!"

"Look. I'm pleased to see you engaging in community activism, Miss Yee. And of course we want our students' voices to be heard. How about holding a bake sale to raise money for art supplies? Or running for student council?"

Whatever. I don't like baking, and student council elections aren't until next September.

This can't be an unsolvable problem.

*Valenti wasn't the one who spent a week watching all
those boys showering in comfort and hanging up their clothes
in big lockers. Valenti doesn't have to lug her running shoes
and shampoo in her backpack every day, when all the supposedly stronger sex have minilockers.*

"Can't we switch?" It comes out of my mouth before I even think about saying it.

"What?"

"Can't you put the girls in the boys' locker room,
starting next fall? We could switch back again halfway
through the year."

"Oh." She wrinkles her brow. "Um. Well, there's
the matter of the bathroom facilities."

"Oh, please. They don't need urinals. They can do
fine in the regular ones."

*Crap,
that came out so sarcastic,
I bet I ruined everything just now—*

Principal Valenti laughs. "You know, Miss Yee, I'm
sure they can." She chuckles again. "Do fine in the regular ones. It's a good idea, actually. I'm surprised no
one thought of it before. How about I run it by Mr.
Sanchez and put it forward at the board meeting this
Wednesday?" she asks.

She said yes,
she said yes,
she said yes!

I stand up and collect my bag from the floor. "Okay. I mean, great. I should get to class now."

"Keep up on your studies, Miss Yee," says Valenti, suddenly strict again. "There's still time to get those grades in shape by the end of the school year. And now that we've met, I'll have my eye on you."

"All right. And thanks."

I walk down the hall in a glow.

Spidey's got nothing on me today.

I'm Gretchen Yee, advocate for equal opportunity and proud wearer of a red vinyl miniskirt.

Housefly no more.

I'm ten minutes late for first-period drawing, and when I get there the whole class has moved the benches so they face one another. Everyone is propping their sketchbooks on their laps and looking carefully at the person across the way. Katya is drawing Brat. Shane is with Malachy. Adrian is with Cammie. Taffy is with that mousy girl Margaret.

Titus is getting ready to draw Kensington, which is

what happens when there's not an even number of people in class. You have to use the teacher as your model. But as soon as Kensington sees me, she stands up and silently gestures that I should get my pad from the storage closet and take her place.

I show her the note from my dad, which now has Principal Valenti's initials on it, and she nods and tells me to sit down. I know the drill. We've done this exercise more than once during the portraiture unit, usually with some variation: the medium we use, or the way we're supposed to look at the subject. I sit down with my pencil box next to me, and peek at what Katya's working with. Vine charcoal.

"Facial portrait," she whispers to me. "Draw the background, too. You're not supposed to take your charcoal off the paper 'cause you're aiming to get a flow going. Start with the inside corner of the eye."

"Got it." I reach over and squeeze her knee.

I get my charcoal out of the box, and flip the sketchbook to a clean page. And now I have to draw Titus.

Titus I've seen without clothes.
Titus I've seen looking in the mirror like he hates himself.
Titus whose dad is gay.
Titus I'm more crazy about than even before I knew this stuff.

And he is going to draw me.
We've never been partners for this exercise before.

I've drawn Katya and Taffy and Malachy, but never Titus, and never Shane. I always avoided it, since I didn't think I'd be able to stand having either one of them look at me for half an hour. It would make me too self-conscious.

And for the first few minutes, I am.

Are my bangs sticking funny to my forehead?
And is my lip gloss still on,
and do I have a pimple on my chin,
or anything on my teeth?

When Katya drew me, I looked round and very Chinese and soft. Her portraits always look warm. When Taffy drew me I looked hard and remote, all sharp edges. Like a shell of a person. And Malachy's was chaotic and precise at the same time—he's good—but he made me look old and worldly, which I'm not.

How will Titus draw me?

I draw the eyes without looking directly at him, the way I draw from the inside of my head when I'm doing comic book stuff. But then I look up, and he's Titus. Still so beautiful, and his right eye is green and purple from the bruise Shane gave him. He's looking down at his paper partly like he's shy and partly like he's thinking hard about what he's doing. And suddenly, I want to see if I can draw him. The way I see him.

Because I know he doesn't see himself as I do.

Charcoal is one of my favorite things to draw with. It's soft, and you can smudge it with your finger to blend, or press hard and get this thick dark line that's very dramatic. I move from his eyes up to his eyebrows, which are narrow and black, and then I do his hair, which I make inky dark and soft-looking. I forget about the background part of the assignment and concentrate on the dark area under his eyes, on his long thin nose, his soft lips with the bottom one jutting out as he concentrates, the shadows across his neck and the details of the silver key chain he wears around it. His lovely bony collarbone jutting out of his worn T-shirt. And I just think

> *edge of the T-shirt*
> *shadow at the collarbone*
> *neck, neck, shadow under the jaw*
> *he's wonderful*
> *he's wonderful*
> *ear, ear*
> *cheekbone*
> *eyebrows*
> *eyelashes*
> *Titus,*

Titus,
Titus.

I put all my love into the picture, I really do. There are soft gray lines crisscrossing his face, since we're not supposed to lift up the charcoal, and they make him look a little sad, a little trapped. I'm surprised when Kensington says our half hour is over, and we should all stand and walk around the room to see what other people have been doing.

I look up, and there is Titus, looking at me. Looking right at me, like he sees me. Like he's been looking into my soul, stupid as that sounds.

He looks down at his pencil case, getting very busy putting the charcoal away.

Kensington won't be happy with what I did. It still has the bold black comic-book line I like to use, and the stylized shading.

I just like it.

It feels like me.

It's how I draw.

No doubt she will lay into me as usual, will say something loud and humiliating that everyone can hear, because she only seems to like it when I'm fake and obedient and I draw the way she thinks is good, the way I did when I did that horrible self-portrait, week before last.

But news flash:

I no longer care if Kensington likes it.

I no longer care if she says something mean and tells the whole class I'm derivative and I don't make art like what hangs in museums.

I am good at this, at comic book drawing.

I'm good at it and I love it.

It is the way I want to draw.

Which is enough.

Besides, this is New York City. Somewhere, in the offices of DC and Marvel, behind the counters of Forbidden Planet on Thirteenth Street, somewhere—lots of places, even—are other people who love it as much as I do. I just need to find them and not be existing in my tiny world anymore.

We walk around the room, looking at what other people have done. Kensington is giving quiet critiques to people, one at a time. Surprisingly, she doesn't say anything to me at all.

I'm dying to race around the benches to see what Titus drew, but I force myself to move slowly.

I can hear Kensington talking to Adrian about negative space and not projecting preconceived ideas onto the subject but just drawing what you see.

When I finally get to Titus's picture of me, I can't quite believe it.

It's beautiful.

It's me, with my bangs hanging crooked and my collar awry,

but the girl in the drawing is lovely.

Titus never draws people so they look lovely. He's a warts-and-all kind of artist, like he's trying to capture the core of someone's individuality.

But me, he made me lovely. He did the mole on my left cheek and my thin upper lip and the shadows under my eyes. But if I were to look at that picture and not know it was me, I would say that the girl was gorgeous.

And that the artist thought she was too.

In English, Titus sits next to me and it's like he's made out of magnets. I used to think all the time about him touching me, brushing my arm with his by accident. But this time, all I can think about is *me* touching *him*.

It's like everything is different, since I saw all those naked bodies and the picture he drew.

Like now, I don't just know what I want; I also know I have to go after it.

I should be taking notes on what Glazer is saying. Especially since I've missed a week of "Metamorphosis" discussions and I'm sure there's a test coming up. There's a pen in my bag, but I leave it where it is. Instead, I reach across Titus's notebook and snag his extra Rollerball.

"Can I use this?" I whisper, putting my hand on his shoulder even though it's unnecessary.

"Go ahead," he whispers back.

Then in my notebook I doodle a picture of Gregor Samsa as a giant cockroach—antennae waving in distress as he sits on his human bed. I shove it over toward Titus.

When Glazer isn't looking, he writes on my paper: "That's how I look, first thing in the morning."

"Me too," I write.

Thinking about what he must look like—wearing pajamas, eyes heavy with sleep, hair even messier than usual—makes me start to sweat. And then I whisper what I actually think. "I'm sure you look delicious."

He blushes, and smiles,

and looks down at his notes like he's concentrating.

When class is over, I catch up with him in the hall.

Hell, maybe he doesn't like me back.

Maybe he doesn't think I'm beautiful and the picture was just a fluke. Maybe he was trying something new with the way he draws.

But if I never ask for what I want, I may never get it— because I know something about Titus now that I never knew before: he is insecure. He thinks he's skinny and bad at sports (which he is), but he thinks it makes him unattractive. That girls won't like him because he's not built, like Shane, or athletic, like Adrian.

So he may never ask me, even if he likes me.

I have to do something myself.

"Wait up," I say, my hands shaking like I've had too much coffee. He's with Adrian, laughing about some nothing, and he turns to look at me. "What? Sure. Ip, I'll catch you later. I have to talk to Gretchen about something."

Adrian, being who he is, socks Titus on the shoulder and waggles his eyebrows. Which is embarrassing, since he's absolutely right about what's going on—at least from my end. But then he disappears down the hall.

People are swarming around us, rushing to get to class before the next bell, but all of a sudden it's like we're the only two people there.

Me and Titus.
Titus and me.
There isn't much time. I better get it out and get it over with.

"You want to go see a movie with me on Friday?" I ask. "We could get dumplings at this place I know, they're like five for a dollar on the street in Chinatown, and then go to the Angelika?"

I can't read his face. He looks surprised, certainly, but I can't tell what else. Whether he wants to go or not. "What's playing?" he asks.

Hell. I don't know what's playing!
I had it all figured out about the dumplings

and where the theater was
and everything,
but I never checked what's playing.

I take a deep breath. "I don't care," I say. "I just want to see it with you."

Because it's the truth.

I want to go somewhere, anywhere, with him.

And then he's grabbing my hand, and pulling me into a storage room they use for art supplies. And he puts his finger to his lips, and the walls are filled with pads of paper and boxes of colored pencils and jars of paint,

and I'm laughing

and he shuts the door behind us

and leans up against it to stop anyone coming in

and like he's trying to get up his nerve now that he's started something,

before we've ever gone to the dumplings and the movies–

he leans in and kisses me.

His lips are cold. The kiss is soft. He has gum in his mouth, and he stops, and giggles nervously, and takes it out and throws it in the trash can,

and looks like he feels embarrassed to have kissed me with the gum,

but I don't care,

and so now I kiss him,

and he's tall enough that he has to bend down to get to me,

and I put my hand on his neck, which is smooth and warm,

and we kiss for a minute in the storage room,

and I want to run my hands up his shirt suddenly— but I don't.

He pulls away for a second and touches my cheek. "I thought you'd never ask," he whispers.

"I thought I never would either," I say, "but I did."

"Good job," he says, and kisses me again.

And I feel lit up inside, I know it's a cliché, but that's the only way I can say it,

and the bell rings, which means we're late,

and we run, laughing, down the hall,

and I get to math and stand in the doorway a second, watching his scrawny body

tearing down the hall

to whatever he's got next.

acknowledgments

Many, many thanks to Marissa,

who believed in this book when it was just a sketch and then edited it with her enormous brain;

and to Elizabeth,

who always knows just what to do and stands by me when the going is rough.

In addition, thanks

to Zoe for help with naming my characters and for taking me to Kid Robot (where Gretchen gets all her little plastic toys);

to the proprietors of www.spiderfan.org for their excellent site, which I used a lot;

to my drawing teacher at SVA in New York City and to Catherine and Aaron for taking class with me;

to Daniel for a good edit,

and to Ivy for existing.

about the author

e. lockhart is the author of *The Boyfriend List* and its forth-
coming sequel, *The Boy Book*. She first met Spider-Man when watching
the *Electric Company* television show at the age of three, and sub-
scribed to *Spider-Man* comics in her early twenties. She has never
turned into an animal of any sort and her knowledge of the boys' locker
room is purely imaginary.

Visit her on the Web at www.theboyfriendlist.com.